CORNWALL'S W
BY
Mabel Quill

CORNWALL'S WONDERLAND

Published by Mythik Press

New York City, NY

First published circa 1924

Copyright © Mythik Press, 2015

All rights reserved

Except in the United States of America, this book is sold subject to the condition that it shall not, by way of trade or otherwise, be lent, re-sold, hired out, or otherwise circulated without the publisher's prior consent in any form of binding or cover other than that in which it is published and without a similar condition including this condition being imposed on the subsequent purchaser.

ABOUT MYTHIK PRESS

From the moment people first began practicing rituals, they have been creating folk tales and legends to celebrate their past and create a unique cultural identity. **Mythik Press** carries these legacies forward by publishing the greatest stories ever concocted, from King Arthur to the fairy tales of the Brothers Grimm.

PREFACE.

With a vivid recollection of the keen enjoyment I myself found in the strange and wonderful Romances and Legends of Old Cornwall, now so rapidly being forgotten; with a remembrance too of the numerous long and involved paragraphs—even pages—that I skipped, as being prosy or unintelligible, written as they were in a dialect often untranslatable even by a Cornish child, I have here tried to present a few of these tales in simpler form, to suit not only Cornish children, but those of all parts.

M.Q.C.

HOW CORINEUS FOUGHT THE CHIEF OF THE GIANTS.

Long, long ago, when Cornwall was almost a desert land, cold, bleak, and poor, and inhabited only by giants, who had destroyed and eaten all the smaller people, Brutus and Corineus came with a large Trojan army intending to conquer England, or Albion as it was then called, and landed at Plymouth for that purpose.

These two valiant chiefs had heard strange tales of the enormous size of the people in that part of the island, so, like wise generals, before venturing inland themselves, they sent parties of their men to explore, and find out what they could of the inhabitants. The soldiers, who had never heard anything about the giants, went off very full of glee, and courage, thinking, from the miserable look of the country, that they had only some poor half-starved, ignorant savages to hunt out, and subdue.

That was how they started out. They returned nearly scared to death, rushing into camp like madmen, pursued by a troop of hideous monsters all brandishing clubs as big as oak trees, and making the most awful noises you can possibly imagine.

When, though, Brutus and Corineus saw these great creatures they were not in the least frightened, for, you see, they had already heard about them. So they quietly and quickly collected their army, reassured the terrified men, and, before the giants knew what was happening, they marched upon them, and assailed them vigorously with spears and darts.

The giants, who were really not at all brave men, were so frightened at this attack, and at the pain caused by the arrows and spears,—weapons they had never seen before,—that they very soon turned tail and ran for their lives. They made direct for the Dartmoor hills, where they hoped to find shelter and safe hiding-places, and indeed, all did manage to escape except one, and that was the great Gogmagog, the captain, who was so badly injured that he could not run.

When Gogmagog saw his cowardly companions all running away, and leaving him to do the best he could for himself, he bellowed and bellowed with rage and fear until the birds nearly dropped down from the sky with fright. After a while, though, he began to think he had better stop drawing attention to himself, and look about for a means of escape, and this was no slight task, for he could scarcely move a step, and his great big body was not at all easy to conceal. Indeed, the only means he could see open to him was to lie down in one of the great ditches which lay here and there all over the land, and trust to the darkness concealing him until the soldiers had returned to camp.

Alas, though, for poor Gogmagog's plans, the moon was at the full, and every place was almost as light as by day. The Trojan soldiers too were so excited and pleased with their giant-hunting, that they could not bear to give it up and return to camp until they had at least one giant to take back as a trophy. So they prowled here, and prowled there, until at last they caught sight of the great bulky body stretched out in the ditch.

Gogmagog, of course, had no chance of escape, he was surrounded and captured, and bound, and the Trojans, rejoicing greatly, dragged him back a prisoner to their camp on Plymouth Hoe. Here, although he was carefully guarded, he was treated with great kindness, fed bountifully, and nursed until his wounds were healed.

When at last he was quite recovered, Brutus, who was very anxious to come to terms with the giants, discussed with him various ways of settling the question they had come with their army to decide, namely, who should be the possessor of the country. He proposed this plan, and that plan, and the other, but none seemed to please Gogmagog, and while the general talked and talked, and tried to come to terms, Gogmagog just sat stolidly listening, and only opening his great mouth to disagree with the general's proposal. The truth was, the giant had a great idea of his own cunning, and he was trying to think of some way by which he could get the better of the invaders, and yet avoid further battles and discharges of arrows. "For," as he said, "you never knew where you were with they things. They had done for you before you'd got time to turn round. Clubs or fists he was equal to, but he didn't see no fun in they sharp little things that stuck right into you, and wouldn't come out until they was cut out."

Thinking of clubs and fists reminded him of wrestling, which was practised a great deal in Cornwall, even in those days, and very little anywhere else.

"The very thing!" thought the wily giant, for it wasn't likely the Trojans knew anything about it, and even if they did, they were only little bits of chaps compared with himself and the other giants. So, after a time, he proposed to Brutus that they should settle matters by "a scat to wrastling," the best man, of course, to have the country.

Rather to Gogmagog's surprise Brutus agreed at once, and it was quickly settled that the giant himself and the best man in the Trojan army should be the two to try their skill. This man was Corineus, who accepted the challenge instantly.

After this the day was soon fixed, and Gogmagog was allowed to send and tell his friends, and bid them all come to Plymouth to witness the great event. The giants, being assured that no arrows or spears would be used against them, came with alacrity, and both they and the Trojans were in a wild state of excitement which increased and increased as the great day drew near.

At last the longed-for time arrived. A ring was formed on the Hoe, the giants all sitting on one side, and the Trojans on the other, and the struggle began.

Oh, it was a fine sight to see two such men pitted against each other, the giant, the finest of his race, and the splendid, stalwart soldier, the enormous strength of the one faced by the skill and coolness of the other, to see them grapple each other and struggle for the mastery as never men had struggled before in hand-to-hand warfare. Such a sight had never been seen in Cornwall until that day, nor ever will be again. It lasted long, and for long the result was doubtful.

"Th' little un can't hold out much longer, mun," cried one of the giants. "Cap'en's only playing with un yet." But just at that very moment Corineus, who was playing a very clever game, dashed in unexpectedly, caught the giant by the girdle, and grasping it like a vice, shook the astonished and breathless monster with all his might and main. The giant, bewildered and gasping, swayed backwards and forwards at his mercy, at first slightly, then more and more, as he failed to regain his balance, until, gathering all his strength for one last effort, Corineus gave him one tremendous push backwards, and sent him clean over, so that he measured his great length upon the ground, and the country for miles round shook with the force of his fall.

Gogmagog gave one awful groan, which sounded like thunder all over the land, making the giantesses, who were left at home, exclaim nervously, "Oh dear, oh dear, there must be an earthquake somewhere! How very unsettled the country is!"

Gogmagog was so stunned and breathless with his fall, that for some time he could not collect his wits, or get up again, so he lay there moaning and puffing until his hard breathing had lashed the sea into fury. The other giants were too frightened to speak or move, for they were quite certain there was magic being used against them, for strength alone could never have overthrown their 'Cap'en' like that, certainly not the strength of 'a little whipper-snapper like that there Corinoos.'

While, though, they were staring open-mouthed, and the giant, never expecting another attack, lay there still puffing and blowing, and trying to think how he could get off facing his opponent again, Corineus had been gathering up all his power to finish his task, and now, dashing in suddenly on his foe, he seized him by the legs, and dragging him to the edge of the cliff, he sent him, with one mighty push, rolling over and over down the sides of the steep cliff into the sea below.

The fearful roar which broke from the giant's throat as he disappeared, the crashing and thudding of his body as it dashed from point to point of the jagged rocks, made even those hardened savages sicken and turn pale, but worst of all was the crash with which he came to the bottom, where his body struck a rock with such violence that it was dashed into a thousand pieces, and his spouting blood dyed the sea crimson for miles and miles around.

After that all turned away pale and sobered, the soldiers to their camp, the giants to their homes, their cowardly hearts full of terror of these new-comers, and the feasting they had promised themselves by way of keeping up their victory was postponed indefinitely.

So ended the fight between the giant and the Trojan. It was not playing the game, but the giants were too cowardly to demand revenge, or to attempt to punish Corineus, and so the land and all in it fell to the Trojans.

Later, when Brutus had conquered all Albion, and was dividing some of it amongst his chiefs, Corineus begged that he might have the giant country, for he loved hunting the great lumbering fellows, and turning them out of their caves and hiding-places. So it was given to him, and he called it Cornwall, because that was something like his own name, and in time he cleared out all the giants, and in their stead there settled there an honest, manly people, who worked and tilled the land, and dug up tin, and did everything that was good, and honourable and industrious, and this is the kind of people who live there still.

THE GIANT OF ST. MICHAEL'S MOUNT.

I am sure most of you have heard of St. Michael's Mount, the strange, beautiful, mountain island, which rises up out of the sea down by Penzance; a mountain island with a grand old castle crowning its summit, and a picturesque group of cottages nestling at its base.

If you have not, you must coax your parents to take you down there for your next summer holiday, then you will be able to see the Mount, and visit it too. And when you are on it you must think to yourself, "Now I am standing where the Giant Cormoran once stood."

You must look out over the sea, too, which surrounds the giant's Mount, and try to picture to yourself a large forest in the place of it, and the sea six long miles away, for that was how it was in Cormoran's time, until one day the sea rose quite suddenly, a huge mountain of water, and rushing over the six miles of land, covered it and the forests too, even above the tops of the tallest trees. Everything for miles around was swallowed up, except the Mount, which was saved by reason of its great height.

From that day to this the sea has never receded, and St. Michael's Mount has remained an island, completely cut off from the mainland, except at low tide, when you can, if you are quick, just manage to walk across.

Years before this, Cormoran had built up the Mount for a home for himself. When first he came to the spot it was all forest, with one large white rock in the midst of it. As he lay on this rock resting, he made up his mind to build himself a hill here, all of white rocks, like the one on which he reclined, where he could live in safety, and keep an eye on the surrounding country.

It was a big task he had set himself, for all the blocks of granite of which it was to be made, had to be brought from a neighbouring hill, those close by being of the pink, or green, or grey kinds, and he would have none of these. Perhaps he would have changed his mind about it had he had to carry all the stone himself, but he, the great lazy fellow, made his wife Cornelian fetch all the heaviest blocks, while he lay idly by and watched her.

Cornelian, who thought the work was very hard indeed, did not see why the green rocks would not do as well as the white, they would be even prettier, in her opinion, so one day when her husband was asleep she knocked off a great green rock, and picking it up in her apron, hurried back as fast as she could to get it fixed in its place before he should wake. She could not manage it though, poor soul, for just as she was reaching her destination the giant opened his eyes, and as soon as he had opened them he caught sight of the green rock she was carrying. Then, oh, what a temper he was in at being disobeyed! He did not say anything, but he got quietly up from his resting-place as soon as she had passed, and followed her, but so softly that she did not notice anything until he was close to her, when he gave her such a blow that she fell staggering under it. Her apron-strings broke, down fell the green stone to the ground, and there it has stayed from that day to this, for no human power has been able to move it.

Cormoran was an old giant, and a very ugly one. He had only one eye, and that was in the middle of his forehead; he had lost nearly all his teeth, too. It would have been better for his appearance had he lost them quite all, for those that were left were broken, jagged, and discoloured, and were anything but ornamental. He was a perfect monster to look at, and, oh, he was such a dreadful thief! All the people who lived anywhere near him went in terror of him, for when he was hungry he would just cross to the mainland, steal the very best cow or sheep in the neighbourhood, sling it across his shoulders and go home with it. And as he was very often hungry, the poor farmer folks were nearly eaten out of house and home by the bad old giant.

On the Pengerswick estate near by, there were some particularly good cattle, which Master Cormoran had taken a great fancy to, and to which he helped himself pretty freely without ever being caught, or punished. Of course, the more he stole the bolder he got, for having so often got off scot-free, he grew to think he was always going to get off scot-free, and that was where he made his mistake.

One day he took it into his head that he would very much like another of these fine, choice animals, so picking up a rope he started off, and wading across to Pengerswick Cove, landed there as usual, thinking he was going to help himself without any trouble and be home again by dinner-time.

It happened, though, that the Lord of Pengerswick had just returned from the East, where he had been learning all sorts of magic and spells. Cormoran, however, knew nothing of this, and if he had he would probably only have laughed and sneered, and turned up his great nose in scorn, for he believed in nothing but giants, and only in two of them,—himself, and the Trecrobben Hill giant.

As Master Cormoran approached, the Lord of Pengerswick, who knew by means of magic all about his coming, and knowing his thieving ways, determined to punish the old thief for all the mischief he had done during his absence. So he began at once to work his spells, meaning to give the giant a very unpleasant time.

Cormoran, never dreaming of any trouble in store for him, landed as usual; but, somehow, when he reached the Cove he did not feel very well, his head felt muzzy and confused: he thought perhaps the sun had been too much for him as he came along. Instead, too, of catching one of the cattle at once, as usual, he had the works of the world to get one, the beasts seemed as slippery as eels, and he was so dull in the head, he hardly knew what he was about. However, after a great deal of trouble, and losing his temper more than once, he managed to catch a fine calf, and tying its four feet together, he slung it round his neck, and prepared to hurry back to the Mount to have a good feast.

He walked, and he walked, and he walked as fast as his feet could carry him, but though he went very quickly, and it was really no distance back to the Cove, he somehow could not get any nearer to the end of his journey; the path seemed all strange to him, too, and for the life of him he could not tell where he was.

At last, when he was so tired that he was ready to drop, he came in sight of a great black rock in Pengerswick Cove. It was a rock he did not remember seeing before, and thinking he was once again on the wrong path he turned to go back. But this, he found to his surprise, was what he could not do. The rock, as if by magic, was drawing him nearer and nearer. It was like a magnet, and struggle as he would, he could not keep away from it. He tried to turn round, he tried to draw back, he even lay down on the ground and dug his heels with all his strength into the sand. But still he felt himself being drawn on and on until he actually touched the rock, and the moment he touched it he found to his horror that he was fastened to it as though by iron bands.

Oh, how he struggled to get free, how he twisted and turned, and kicked! All in vain, though. He might as well have lain still and gone to sleep for all the good he did. By degrees, too, he felt himself growing more and more helpless, he could not move hand or foot, he grew colder and stiffer, and stiffer and colder, until at last he was as if turned to stone, except that his senses were more acute than ever they had been before. To add to his torments, too, the calf which he had slung across his shoulders, struggled and kicked and bellowed until the old thief was black and blue, and nearly deafened. He was nearly scared to death, too, for fear someone would hear the creature's noise, and come in search of it, to find out what was the matter.

He tried and tried to throw off his burden, but nothing would loosen it, and all the night long he had to bear the bleating and the bellowing in his ear, and the incessant kicking and butting, for, for the whole of the night the giant had to remain there; and probably he would have been there for the rest of his life, had not the Lord of Pengerswick thought he would like to have some more fun with him.

Early in the morning the Enchanter mounted his horse and rode down to the Cove to have a look at Master Cormoran, and to give him a piece of his mind before he removed the spell and let him go, and a piece of something else as well! Cormoran quaked when he saw the old lord coming, for he looked every bit as angry as he really was, and first he lashed the giant with his tongue, and then he lashed him with his whip, and he flogged him and flogged him until in his agony Cormoran kicked and struggled so hard that he broke away from the rock and leaped right into the sea.

This was the way the Enchanter removed the spell!

Once free from that terrible rock, Cormoran soon reached home, but the lesson he had had was one that he never forgot, and he never troubled that part of the country again, so the people all around had good cause to thank the Lord of Pengerswick. Poor Cornelian, his wife, had a sad time of it, though, for so sore was the giant from his beating, and so angry and mortified, that his temper became something worse than ever. Indeed, I cannot find words to describe it.

Poor Cornelian herself was very kind and good-tempered, and a very hard-working giantess, and she was very much to be pitied for having such a disagreeable, grumpy old husband. Cornelian, though, had one great fault, and that was that she was very, very inquisitive. I do not know that she ever did any harm to anyone but herself by it. It brought about her own death, though, in a very dreadful manner. And this was how it was.

Cormoran and the Trecrobben Hill giant were very friendly and neighbourly one with the other, and they used to borrow and lend to each other any little thing they happened to want, just as ordinary people do who are on very good terms with one another.

One day Cormoran was wanting the cobbling-hammer to mend his boots, but the hammer was up at Trecrobben's,—they only had one between them. So he went out and shouted, "Halloa, up there! Hi! Trecrobben, throw us down the cobblen hammer, wust-a?" They always threw across to each other what they wanted.

"To be sure," called back Trecrobben; "here, look out and catch un!"

Hearing a lot of noise and shouting, Cornelian must needs bustle out to find out what it was all about, and running from the dark house to the bright sunshine, her eyes were so dazzled, she did not see the great hammer coming hurtling through the air, as it did at that very moment, and whack! crack! it caught her a terrible blow right between the eyes, even crashing in the mighty bone of her forehead.

Down she fell with a groan right at her husband's feet, and when he turned her over she was as dead as the fatal hammer itself! Then what a to-do there was! The two giants wept and roared over the corpse, they wrung their hands and tore their hair, but it was all of no use, they could not bring poor Cornelian back to life again. Their sighs and groans only wrecked a ship or two out at sea, and blew the roofs off some houses at Market Jew. So they stopped, and set to work to bury poor Cornelian. They thought it best to get her out of sight as quickly as possible, it made them weep so to see her lying there dead.

Where they laid her, though, no one knows. Some say it was in the court of the castle, others that they lifted Chapel Rock and put her under; but there are others who say that they only rolled her over the edge of the cliffs and into the sea! You will always, though, find some people ready to say unkind things about everyone.

Cormoran himself met his death some years later at the hands of Jack the Giant-Killer, but as you probably know that story, I will not repeat it here.

THE LEGEND OF THE TAMAR, THE TAVY, AND THE TAW.

In the days when fairies, giants, and witches, gnomes and piskies, and dwarfs, and all the other Big People and Little People dwelt on the land or under it, there lived in a huge cavern, deep, deep down in the heart of the earth, two gnomes, husband and wife, busy, practical little people, who spent their lives digging and delving in the very bowels of the earth.

They had no cravings for a more beautiful life, no desire to see the sunshine, the flowers, the green grass, or the wide blue sea. They wanted nothing better, or beyond the life which had always been theirs.

To them, though, there was sent a little daughter, whom they called Tamara. She was a lovely, golden-haired sprite, as unlike her parents as the sun the night, and they were filled with happiness and pride, and wonder of her beauty.

When Tamara was old enough, they would have set her to work with them, but Tamara did not like the cold, dark cavern, or the silence and bareness of her underground home. She was an earth-loving child, and had a passion for the upper world, whither she would escape as often as she possibly could, for the sun, the flowers, the birds, the happy life which surrounded her up there, were a never-failing joy to her.

Her parents scolded and scolded; they warned her that the earth was full of giants, and if she were captured by one of them, nothing could save her; but she paid no heed to them at all, for she did not know what fear was, she could not believe that anyone could harm her. And they had petted and humoured her, and allowed her her own way in so many things, she did not see why she should not do as she liked in this.

She hated the cold, gloomy underground, so why should she stay there, she argued, and she ran away more and more to the upper world, and spent her days in roaming over the moors chasing the birds and butterflies, or, when she was tired, lying on a bank of moss and ferns, gazing up at the glorious sun, and basking in its kindly warmth.

At length one day, Tawridge and Tavy, sons of two Dartmoor giants, met sweet Tamara as she was wandering amongst the furze and bracken, and straightway fell in love with her. They had only seen giantesses up to that time, who, though very fine and striking in appearance, are never pretty, and these two young giants had never in their lives seen anything so delicate and so lovely as Tamara, or dreamed that it was possible that such beautiful maidens could exist.

Straightway each of them lost his great big heart to the dainty maiden, and could not bear to lose sight of her. So afraid were they that she would vanish, and they would never see her again, that they followed her far and wide over the moor, trying to coax her to come and talk with them. But Tamara, like a laughing, mischievous sprite, ran from them laughing, led them over moor and river, always evading them, never letting them reach her. The more though that she tantalized and teased them, the more the poor fellows loved her, and they sighed for her until their great hearts were like to break.

One morning, Tamara got away earlier than usual from her cavern home. She awoke long before her parents, and after gazing for some time at the darkness which filled the cave, and shivering in the chill, damp air, she thought of the upper world where the morning sun would be shining on the dewy grass, and the birds be singing their first glad song; and as she pictured it all the longing to be up there grew stronger than she could bear. She rose quietly, and without disturbing her parents, left her home for the last time.

In the upper world all was as she had pictured it, and lost in the joy and beauty of it, Tamara wandered on and on until she came to a place called Morwenstow, and a dainty little pool in the hollow of a rock. The sun was so warm, and the pool so lovely, Tamara felt she must step into it; so, laying aside her robe, she played and swam about in the fresh clear water until she was quite tired out, when she dressed herself in her robe again, and shaking her long golden locks to dry them, she lay down under the shelter of a hawthorn-bush, and soon fell fast asleep.

Ah me! how sweet she looked, with her delicate cheeks so rosy after her bathe, her lovely lashes resting on them, her cloud of golden hair spread all about her! and so thought Tavy and Tawridge when they came along and found her! At the sight of her they stood speechless with admiration, but the great stupid fellows were as quiet and careful not to waken her as fairies would have been. They just sat down near her and gazed and gazed at her with great faithful dog-like eyes.

Presently a thrush began to sing hard by, and with a little stretch and a sleepy sigh Tamara opened her big blue eyes. When she caught sight of her guardians and captors, she broke into a little rippling laugh and sprang to her feet, but this time she could not escape.

"Do not leave us," they pleaded. "We will not hurt you, Tamara. We may be big and ugly, but we have good hearts. Have pity on us, lovely one, for you know how we worship you, and how our lives are spent in seeking you. Such a love for you fills our hearts we know no rest away from you."

They pleaded long and earnestly, those two love-stricken giants, they called her by every sweet and endearing name that they could think of, and Tamara listened, and made no further attempt to run away. Their devotion pleased her, it was so new and strange, and she loved to feel her power. So the morning sped away.

Deep down in the dark earth, the industrious little gnomes paused in their labours and wondered where Tamara was. "She does not often stay so long," said the mother; "I trust no harm has befallen her."

"What a trouble she is to us!" said the father, growing angry because he was alarmed. "We should be glad we have no more children, or we should have to spend all our time looking after them, to see they came to no harm. We should never have time for our work, and never know peace of mind."

"Yes, yes," said the mother impatiently, "but Tamara! Where can she be? The earth is full of giants, and I am full of fears. I cannot rest, I must go and seek her, and you must come too. She is so beautiful, and so thoughtless and full of life."

So they mounted to the upper world, and began their weary search for their naughty little daughter; and by and by they found her seated on a couch of sweet, soft heather, between the two giants. They were still telling her of their love for her,—there was so much, it took long to tell,—

and beseeching her to choose one of them for her own faithful lover.

The father gnome was very much alarmed at this sight, for what could he, no taller than a tulip, do against two such monstrous creatures? Their thumbs alone were as big as his whole body. All that was left to be done was to appeal to Tamara, and each in turn, and both together, the father and mother begged and commanded their runaway child to return to her home.

But Tamara was as obstinate as could be. "No, I want to stay here," she said, "these good boys love me, and they will break their hearts when I leave them. You would not have me make them so unhappy, would you? I want, too, to hear all about their country and their people, for I love it, and I love them, and I hate the cold, dark cavern, with its eternal work, work, work!" Then she turned entreatingly to the giants, "You will not let me be taken back, will you?" she cried, her beautiful eyes full of appealing.

"No, no!" they cried joyfully, "we will take care of you, little Tamara."

Even, though, as they spoke, a deep sleep fell upon them. The gnome, thoroughly angry, had cast a spell upon them, and poor Tamara saw herself in an instant deprived of both her protectors. She was deeply mortified, but more determined than ever not to go back to her dark, gloomy home. No pleadings, or coaxings, or commands had any power to move her. Her mother appealed to her, her father scolded, all in vain. Anger was roused on both sides, until at length in ungovernable rage the father cursed his daughter, and as his curse fell on her, the weeping girl was changed into a crystal stream, which soon became a river; a beautiful, rapid river, for ever winding its way with a low, sad murmur, in storm or sunshine, through the land she loved so well, on and on to the great salt ocean.

The angry parents, heartbroken and desolate, had returned to their lonely home, and Tamara, with low, sad sighs, was fleeing further and further from her sleeping lovers, when Tavy at last awoke. He sat up and glared around him, too dazed to realize at first all that had happened. He looked at Tawridge, lying fast asleep, and recollection began to return,—he looked for Tamara,—she was gone!

In a frenzy of fear lest he should have lost his new-found love for ever, he rushed hither and thither, wildly searching for her,—but, of course, in vain.

"Tamara! Tamara!" he called despairingly; no answer came. No sound reached him but the sweet, sad voice of a stream hard by, a stream he did not remember to have heard before. He was too full of his troubles, though, to pay heed to such trifles now.

Flying as fast as the wind to his father amongst the hills, he told him his pitiful tale, but the giant already knew all that had happened, for he had powers his son had not.

"My boy," he said sadly, "your Tamara is gone. Cruelly taken from you. I cannot bring her back to you, but I can send you to her. Grieved I shall be to lose my son, but I cannot keep you here and see your life filled with endless pain." Then the old giant kissed his son, and as he kissed him he turned him into a stream, which, noisy and turbulent as poor Tavy himself had been of old, rushed madly on over rock and moor, seeking his lost love. Wildly he dashed ahead, seeking to overtake her, until at last in a gentle valley where she loitered slowly, he came upon her, and, happy that they had met at last, hand in hand they glided softly onwards to the eternal sea.

During all this time poor Tawridge slept on, dreaming of Tamara, that she was his, and nothing could part them; but alas, alas for his waking! He opened his eyes and found it was but a dream! Tamara was gone, Tavy was gone, and he was left alone.

"They have gone together!" was his first thought, but then he remembered the arrival of the father and mother, and his second thought was that Tamara had been taken back to her home by her parents, and that Tavy had killed himself in despair. And Tawridge was filled with a double grief, for he had really loved poor Tavy.

In the hills there lived an Enchanter, and to him Tawridge ran for help, and of him he learnt the truth,—that both were lost to him, and were together. The knowledge drove him to frenzy. Without a thought for his father or mother, or anyone else who loved him, he begged and implored the Enchanter to turn him into a stream too, that he might follow the others and overtake them, and once again be with his lost love, or near her.

At last the old Enchanter consented, and Tawridge was turned into a swiftly flowing river; and there his troubles might have ended, and the three friends have been reunited, but, as he was going back, Tawridge mistook the way, and, instead of flowing towards the sea with Tamara and Tavy, he rushed on wildly seeking them in the wrong direction. Calling to them with heartbroken cries and moans, he hurried faster and faster in his longing to overtake them, but always in the wrong direction, ever and ever flowing farther from them, never to meet his lost love again.

To this day the Tamar and the Tavy run always side by side, and the Taw, still sighing and moaning sadly, rushes in the opposite direction, and never can the enchantment be removed from Tamara and her lovers, until we, having grown better and wiser, become friends again with the Big People and the Little People we have driven from us by our ignorance and narrow minds.

THE STRANGE STORY OF CHERRY HONEY.

Cherry Honey, with her father and mother, and a half-score of brothers and sisters, lived in a little hut at Trereen, in the parish of Zennor. They were very poor people, terribly poor, for all they had to live on was what they could get out of a few acres of ground that they owned,—ground as barren as any you could find thereabouts, and that is saying a good deal. For food they lived mostly on fish and potatoes, except on Sundays, when they had pork, and the broth it was boiled in; and twice a year, at Christmas and Feast-day, they had, as a great luxury, white bread.

Whether fish and potatoes make people strong, or whether the air at Trereen was specially good, I can't tell, but sure enough it is that all Tom Honey's children grew up into fine, handsome men and women, and not one weakly one amongst them.

They were a lively crew too, as merry as grigs in spite of the cold and the hunger that they felt pretty often, and the liveliest and merriest of the lot was Cherry. She was full of pranks and mischief, and led the others a pretty life. When the miller's boy came to know if they wanted to send any corn to be ground, Cherry would slip out, mount his horse, which he left fastened up close by, and off she would go, racing as hard as she could go all along the very edge of the cliff, and away to the Downs, the miller's boy racing and yelling after her, but he might as well have tried to catch a will-o'-the-wisp.

So Cherry went on very happily, working very hard and playing too, until she reached the age of sixteen or so, when she began to feel a wish to see more life than that lonely moor provided, and have a change from the tiny hut which could not hold a half of them comfortably. She wanted a new gown too, her mother had promised it to her ever since she was thirteen, and she had looked forward to it even more than she did to Feasten-Sunday, for she had never had a new frock in her life. She could not enjoy Feasten-Sunday either, unless she was dressed as nicely as other girls.

Year after year, though, she was disappointed, there was no money and no new dress, and poor Cherry had to content herself with a clean apron over her shabby old frock, which had been patched and mended until there was only one piece of the original left, and no one but Cherry herself could have told which that was.

She was not fit to go to church or to fair, and she felt it very hard that she could never enjoy herself. And then, to make matters worse, her great friend Tamsin Bray, who was a year younger than Cherry, had a beautiful frock all trimmed with ribbons, and she wore it to Nancledry to the preaching there, and had a fine time there, full of adventures and new experiences, as she took care to tell poor Cherry when she came back, making Cherry feel more dissatisfied than ever. She knew she was a prettier girl than Tamsin, and would get more admiration if she only had the chance.

After that Cherry could no longer go on bearing things as they were. If her mother couldn't buy her a new frock, she would go to work, and earn one for herself, she determined. So she told her parents she was going to look for a situation, and nothing they could say could make her change her mind, so they gave up trying to.

"Why don't 'ee try and get a place down to Towednack?" asked her mother, who wanted her not to go far from home.

"Iss, fay, mother," answered Cherry sharply, "a likely tale I'm going to live in a place where the cow ate the bell-rope, and where they've nothing but fish and taties all the year round, except Sundays, when they have conger-pie! Dear no, I'm going where I can get butcher's meat sometimes, and a bit of saffern cake when I wants it!"

So Cherry packed up her few garments, which made but a very small bundle, and started off, after promising her father not to go too far, and to come home soon. She had been so restless and uneasy, that the poor man thought she was bewitched, or something. He feared, too, that she might get carried off by pirates, for there were many of them about Cornwall in those days, and Cherry was an attractive-looking girl, and rather flighty, as her mother often said.

When Cherry had said 'good-bye' and kissed them all, and got outside, she had not the slightest notion which way to go, so she took the road to Ludgvan and Gulval, and walked on briskly enough for a time; but when she turned round for a last look at the old home, and found that it was no longer in sight, she felt so miserable that she had a very good mind to turn round and go back. It was the first time she had ever been away, and she felt very home-sick and lonesome. Indeed, the outlook was enough to damp her spirits and even frighten her, for she had no friends to go to, nor a situation. She did not even know where she should find shelter that night, and she had only one penny in her pocket. However, she started on again, and trudged along the lonely road until she came to the four cross-roads on the Lady Downs.

Here she paused again, and rested while she tried to make up her mind which of the four roads she should take. All around her the Downs stretched, looking bleak and wild; and all the stories she had ever heard of highwaymen and pirates, witches and fairies, came rushing helter-skelter through her poor brain until she felt too terrified to walk on or to turn back; and at last she sat down on a big stone by the side of the road and burst out crying.

She did cry too, most bitterly, and never stopped until she had made up her mind to retrace her steps, and go home as fast as she could go. Having settled that, she felt much happier, and drying her eyes she started up, only too anxious to get out of that great wilderness. She wondered if her brothers and sisters would laugh at her. Yes, she felt sure that they would, but she did not care, she told herself. She would soon play them some trick that would make them laugh the other side of their faces. Her father and mother would welcome her back gladly, she knew.

So she turned her face towards home, and was trying not to feel ashamed of her want of pluck,—when she saw a gentleman on the road just ahead of her, and walking towards her. She was astonished, and just a little alarmed, for a moment before there was not a soul to be seen. She was so astonished that she quite forgot her manners, and stood staring and staring at the gentleman until he had come quite close to her. Then he stared hard at Cherry, but it was not a rude stare, and he took off his hat so politely, and smiled so pleasantly, that Cherry was quite impressed.

"Can you tell me the way to Towednack?" he asked in a voice as pleasant as his smile.

"Yes, sir," answered Cherry, curtseying. "If you'll please to walk a little way with me, sir, I'll put you in the right road."

The gentleman thanked her, and as he walked along beside her, he asked which way she was going, and where she lived, and he was so kind and had such a pleasant way with him, that Cherry had soon told him her history, and how she had left home to go to look for a 'place,' and how she had felt so lonesome on the Downs, and so home-sick, that she had changed her mind and was going straight back again.

"Well, this is strange!" exclaimed the gentleman. "Of all the good luck this is the greatest! I have come out to-day to see if I can find a good active girl in one of the villages, for I want a servant; and here I find just what I am looking for, a handsome, sharp young woman, cleanly and honest."

He could judge for himself what sort of a girl Cherry was, by her appearance, and her clean, well-mended frock.

He went on to tell her that he was a widower with one little boy, for whom he wanted a nurse, and would Cherry come and take the post?

He talked for a long time very earnestly and winningly. Cherry did not understand a half that he said, but she understood enough to make her feel that this would be a better situation for her than she had ever dreamed of getting, and before very long she consented to go.

The gentleman seemed very pleased, and away they started together at once, the stranger talking very fast all the time, and making himself so entertaining that Cherry never noticed how far they were going, nor in what direction.

They walked through such beautiful lanes that it was quite a pleasure to be in them, hung as they were with honeysuckles and roses, and many other beautiful flowers, such as Cherry rarely saw anywhere near her bleak home.

By and by the light began to fail, which rather surprised Cherry, who had no idea the day was so far gone. She had no watch or means of telling the time, so she supposed it was all right, and that she had sat crying longer than she thought. Presently they came to a river, and Cherry wondered how she should cross it, for it had grown so dark by that time she could not see stepping-stones, or bridge, or anything.

However, while she was wondering, the gentleman just picked her up in his arms and carried her across, and then on they walked again. They went down, down and down a very steep lane now, a lane which got narrower and narrower, and was so steep and long, Cherry thought it would never end. Not that she minded much, for she did not feel tired, and the gentleman had given her his arm, that she might not stumble, and she felt so excited and happy she could have walked on through the sweet-scented darkness for ever.

She had not much further to go, though, for presently they came to a gate which the gentleman opened. "This is your new home, Cherry," he said kindly, and Cherry found herself suddenly in the most beautiful garden you can imagine. It was full of lovely flowers and luscious fruits, while flitting about everywhere, or perching on the trees, were birds of all sizes and colours, tiny blue birds, large scarlet birds, some that flashed like silver, and gold, and beaten copper, in the sunlight. For oddly enough the sun was shining brightly in the garden, though it had long been dark outside.

Cherry stood and stared about her in open-eyed amazement. "Dear, dear," she thought to herself, "'tis just like the fairy-tales Gammer tells us winter evenings!" and she began to wonder if she could have got into an enchanted place, and if she should presently see fairies, or enchanted people there. But no, it could not be any fairy-tale, for there was her new master standing by her as big as Farmer Chenoweth, and down the path came running a little boy, calling "Papa! papa!" just as any ordinary mortal child would.

Though, as Cherry said afterwards, there was something uncanny about the child, for he had such an odd, old face and expression, and eyes as cunning as might be, and so bright and piercing they seemed to look you through and through; yet he appeared to be no more than four years old.

Before the child could reach them, an old woman came running out after him, and seizing him by the arm dragged him roughly back to the house. She was a bony, ill-tempered looking old woman, and before she retired, grumbling at the child and shaking him, she favoured Cherry with such an evil glance that the poor girl felt more than half inclined to turn and run right away.

"That's my late wife's grandmother," explained the widower; "she is a cross-grained old catamaran, and the reason she eyed you so unpleasantly is that she knows I have brought you here to take her place. Make haste and learn your work, Cherry, for I want to send the cross old dame about her business," which was hardly a respectful way in which to speak of his grandmother-in-law.

He took Cherry into the house, which was even more beautiful than the garden; brilliant light, like sunshine, lighted up every room, flowers grew everywhere, mirrors and pictures lined the walls, and as for the ornaments, the carpets, curtains and other beautiful things, you could never believe what their beauty was unless you could see them.

"It is all so grand," said Cherry to herself, "'tis too much to take in all at once. It makes my head swim, and I'd like something to eat for a change." She was really very, very hungry, for she had had nothing to eat all day but a slice of bread and treacle.

Hardly had the thought come into her head, when Aunt Prudence,—as the old grandmother was called,—began to lay a table with all kinds of delicious food, to which she bade Cherry sit down and eat.

Cherry did not require a second bidding, you may be quite sure, nor did she stop until she had made a very good meal indeed. After that she was told her duties. She was to sleep in the room with the child, and in the morning to take him and bathe him in a spring in the garden. After she had bathed him she was to anoint his eyes with some ointment she would find in a little box in a cleft in the rock. She was to be very careful indeed to put the little box back where she took it from, and on no account to touch her own eyes with it. After that was all done she was to milk the cow, and give the child a basin of the last milk she drew.

You can imagine how all this raised Cherry's curiosity, and how she longed to get the little boy to tell her about everything, but, as he always threatened to tell Aunt Prudence, directly she asked him a question, she thought it better to hold her tongue, and try to find out things for herself.

When she had been told all her duties, she was conducted to her room by the old lady, who bade her keep her eyes shut, whether she was asleep or not, or she might wish too late that she had. She forbade her, too, to talk to the child about anything. So Cherry was rather frightened by the time she got to bed, and until she fell asleep she kept her eyes and her mouth fast closed, but fortunately, thanks to her tiring day and her good supper, she did not stay awake long.

The next morning as soon as she was awake she got up and began her work, but when she had bathed the boy in the stream to which he led her, and had put the ointment on his eyes, she did not know how to set about her next task, for there was not a cow to be seen anywhere.

"Call her," said the boy, when she told him her trouble. So Cherry called, "Coo-o, coo-o, coo-o-o," just as she did at home, and at once a pretty sleek cow came from somewhere,—it might have been out of the ground, as far as Cherry could tell. Anyhow, there she was, and Cherry sat down and milked her, and gave the boy his breakfast, and when she had done the cow walked away again and disappeared.

After that Cherry went indoors, where the Grandmother provided her with a big breakfast all to herself, after which she told her of some more of her duties. Cherry was to keep in the kitchen, and clean the pots and pans with water and sand, scald the milk, make the butter, and do anything else she was told. Above all she was to avoid curiosity, to keep to the kitchen, and never try to enter or look into a room that was locked.

Cherry felt that this was very hard, for, as I said before, she was full of curiosity, and wanted to find out all she could about these strange people she had got amongst. She could scarcely endure old Aunt Prudence with her scoldings and growlings, for the old woman never ceased grumbling at both the girl and her grandson-in-law for bringing her there.

"I knew Robin would bring some stupid thing from Zennor," she would say, and she would scowl at Cherry until the girl grew quite nervous. She tried to get as far away from the old woman as she could, but, as Cherry said, the old soul seemed to have eyes all over her head, for she always had one on Cherry, no matter where she was or what she was doing.

The happiest time of Cherry's life here was when her housework was done, and her master called to her to come and help him in the garden; for he was always kind and gentle to her, and always rewarded her with a word of praise.

Aunt Prudence, though, was not always a cross old tyrant; she had her kinder moods, and in one of them she told Cherry that if she was a good girl, and did her work quickly, she would take her into those parts of the house where she had been forbidden to go, and show her some of the wonderful sights of the place!

Oh, how delighted Cherry was, and how she did hurry through her work! She felt that now she was going to be made happy for the rest of her life, and would have nothing left to wish for. She got through her work so quickly, that it was still quite early when they started off together on their sight-seeing.

First of all they came to a door opening out of a passage, and here Aunt Prudence told Cherry to take off her shoes. This done, they opened the door and entered, letting it fall silently behind them. The passage was very low and very dark, and Cherry, who had to feel her way by the wall, felt rather nervous, for she could not see where her next step would take her. Before very long, though, they came to a room where the light was bright, it was a beautiful room, with a floor like glass, but, oh, how frightened Cherry was when she stepped into it! for ranged all round the walls, on shelves or on the floor, were a lot of people turned to stone. Some had no arms, others no legs, while of others there were only the head and shoulders. Some heads had no ears, others had no noses, and some few were without either.

Oh, it was a horrid sight, and Cherry was terribly frightened lest they should all come to life suddenly, and set on her and tear off her limbs too. She told Aunt Prudence, "she was mortal fear't of 'em, for she'd heard tell on 'em up to Zennor, and everybody said there was never no knowing what they wouldn't be up to. She'd thought all along that she'd got in with the Little People, only her master was such a fine upstanding man, she'd never have took him for a fairy."

Aunt Prudence only laughed at her, and seeing that she really was afraid, took a greater pleasure in making her go further. There was a curious-looking thing standing in the room, like a coffin on six legs, and this Aunt Prudence insisted on Cherry's giving a good polishing to. So Cherry had to set to and rub it with all her might and main, for she dared not disobey the old lady; but the more she rubbed the more the old lady scolded her to rub harder, and Cherry rubbed harder and harder and harder, until at last she nearly upset the thing. She threw out her arms and seized, but as it tottered it gave out the most soul-piercing, unearthly yell it was possible for anyone ever to hear.

"They'm coming to life! They'm coming to life!" shrieked out Cherry, and from sheer fright she fell on the floor in a fit.

All this noise and uproar reached the master's ears, and up he came, to know what it was all about. And oh, he was angry when he found out. First of all he ordered old Aunt Prudence out of the house then and there, and then he picked up Cherry and carried her to the kitchen, where he soon brought her to her senses again, but, strangely enough, she could not remember what had happened, or why she was there. Her memory of what she had seen had quite gone, and though she was always afraid, after that, to go into that part of the house again, she could not remember in the least why it was, or anything that had happened there.

Cherry felt much happier now, and did not worry herself about it, for Aunt Prudence and her terrifying eye were gone, and she was left sole mistress. So time passed on, and Cherry's master was so kind to her that the days flew by like hours, and very soon a whole year was gone.

During all this time she had never once thought of her home, or her parents, or her old life. She had everything she could wish, and you would have thought she was bound to be happy; but no, nothing of the sort! She soon grew accustomed to her happiness, and then she began to want the things she had not got. Her curiosity increased every day. She longed to know more about the mysterious part of the house, and a hundred other things that she should never have troubled her head about.

She was particularly anxious to find out all about her master, for his movements were certainly very strange, and puzzled Cherry. He went off every morning soon after his early breakfast, and when he came back he shut himself into the room where the stone figures were, and Cherry was certain, for she had crept up and listened at the door, that she could hear him talking to them!

What could she do to get to know more, she wondered. She thought and thought, and then one day her thoughts flew to the ointment. She had often noticed how very bright and peculiar the little boy's eyes became after she had anointed them, and that he often seemed able to see things that were hidden from her.

Cherry grew very excited, she felt sure she had discovered the secret. So the next morning, after she had bathed him and given him his breakfast, she sent him away to play for a few minutes, and whisking out the ointment pot again, she brushed the least bit of it over one of her eyes with the tip of her finger.

Oh, how it burned and smarted! and oh, how she did rub her eye and try to get the nasty stuff out! But it would not come. She ran to the stream and knelt down to bathe it,—and as she knelt and looked in the water she saw, at the very bottom, dozens and dozens of little people, playing and dancing, and enjoying themselves as though they were on dry land. And there, too, as gay as any, and as small as any, was her master himself. Bewildered and frightened, Cherry sprang to her feet, but as she turned to run she saw everything was changed. There were Little People everywhere, hanging on the trees overhead, swarming over the ground at her feet, swinging on the flowers, some astride the stalks, others curled up in the cups, all exquisitely dressed, and flashing with gold and jewels; and all as merry as crickets.

Cherry thought she was bewitched sure enough, and she was so frightened she did not know what to do.

At night back rode her master, as big and handsome as ever, and very unlike the little piskyman she had seen at the bottom of the water. He went straight up to the locked-up room where the stone figures were, and very soon Cherry heard sounds of most lovely music issuing thence. So things went on day after day, the widower rode off every morning dressed as any ordinary gentleman would be to follow the hounds, and never came back again until night, when he retired at once to his own rooms.

All this was almost too much for poor Cherry's brain. She felt that if she did not find out more, she should die of curiosity. Knowing so much only made her long to know more.

At last, one night after her master had gone to the enchanted room, Cherry crept up to the door, and instead of only listening at it as usual, she knelt down and peeped through the keyhole, which, for once, was not covered.

Inside the room she saw her master in the midst of a number of ladies, some of whom were singing, and their voices sounded like silver bells; others were walking about, but one, the most beautiful of all, was sitting at the coffin on six legs, performing on it as though it were a piano. She had long dark hair streaming right down to the floor, and a blue gown all trimmed with sparkling silver, her shoes were blue with diamond stars on the toes, and round her neck she had a string of turquoises set in diamonds.

Poor Cherry was very much hurt and mortified when she saw her beloved master with all those lovely ladies, but oh, how miserable she felt when she saw him kiss the lovely lady in blue and silver! She did not say anything, though,—indeed, she had no one to speak to,—and she went about her work as usual, but the next morning when her master came into the garden and began to talk to her as usual she answered him quite shortly and rudely, and when he asked her what was the matter with her, she told him to leave her to herself. If he wanted to talk he could go and talk to the Little People he was so fond of.

Her master was very much surprised and annoyed when he heard this, for he knew that she had been disobedient, and had used the Fairy Ointment. He did not scold her, though, but he told her simply and mournfully, and in a tone which gave her no hope, that they must part.

"You will have to go home, Cherry; you have disobeyed my orders. I can have no one spying and watching me. I must send you away, my child." He spoke so sadly that Cherry's heart felt as though it must break. "And I must have Aunt Prudence back," he added, with a sigh.

Very, very unhappy was poor Cherry when she went to bed that night, and she had only just cried herself to sleep when her master came and woke her, telling her to get up and dress. Without a word, but choked with sobs, she obeyed him, and when she was ready she found him waiting for her, with a lantern and a large bundle of beautiful clothes that he had tied up for her.

As soon as they had had some food they started, and miles and miles and miles they walked, for the way seemed ten times as long as when they came. For one thing it was all uphill now, and for another, Cherry's heart was heavy, and a heavy heart makes heavy feet.

It was nearly daybreak when at last they reached the Lady Downs, and came to a standstill. The sun was just rising over the great lonely moor.

"We must part now, my poor child," said her master. "You are severely punished for your curiosity, but it cannot be otherwise. Good-bye, Cherry; do your duty, and try to get the better of your failing, and if you are a good girl I will come to these Downs sometimes to see you."

Then kissing her, he turned away and disappeared as suddenly as he had first appeared.

Dazed and stupefied, scarcely able to realize all the trouble that had befallen her, Cherry sat for a long time where he had left her. In her thoughts she went over and over her happy life for the past year, all that she had had, and lost. By and by the sun came out in its full strength and warmed her, and roused her sufficiently to look about her, and wonder what she should do next, for, of course, she could not stay where she was.

Presently she noticed that she was sitting on the very same stone at the cross-roads where, on the day she left home, she had sat and cried, and the strange gentleman had first appeared to her. The recollection brought back to her more painfully than ever her own foolishness and wickedness, and all that she had lost, and oh, how miserable she did feel, and how she cried and cried, and how she longed and longed for her dear, good master to come again and forgive her.

He did not come, though, and by and by, as the day had worn far on, Cherry felt that she had better seek her home before nightfall. Listlessly enough she rose and trudged along the old familiar roads to her father's house, with miserable eyes she recognized the old landmarks, but without any pleasure, until at last she came to the poor little hut she called 'home.' It looked poorer, and meaner, and more comfortless than ever, after the luxuries she had grown accustomed to. Her mother and all the rest of them were sitting at dinner when Cherry opened the door. At the sound of the latch Mrs. Honey looked up, and gave one big screech.

"Why, 'tis Cherry!" she cried, "or her ghost! Cross her, father. Cross her!" And when Cherry, taking no notice of her screams, advanced into the kitchen, they all backed away from her, one on top of another, each trying to get behind someone else, for they had long since made up their minds that Cherry was dead, and never for a moment dreamed that this apparition was Cherry herself, living flesh and blood.

Not until she flopped into a chair, saying wearily, "Give me a dish of tay, mother, for goodness sake, I'm so wisht I don't know how to bear with myself."

"Tisn't no ghost, mother," cried Tom Honey, his courage reviving; "no ghost would want such poor trade as tay."

Then the others plucked up their spirits, too, and crowded round her, asking a dozen questions, and all at the same time; and for the sake of peace and quiet Cherry told them her wonderful adventures from the day she left them, and, as was to be expected, not one believed a word of it.

"The maid's mazed," said her father, and the others agreed. But as time went on Cherry repeated the tale so often, and always the same; and she cried so bitterly for her master and his little boy, that they were obliged to believe her, in spite of themselves. "There must be some truth in it," they said, "it couldn't all be fancy."

Poor Cherry! She was never happy again after her experience. Many people said she was bewitched, others declared she was wrong in her mind, but that was only because whenever there was a moonlight night, she wandered on the Lady Downs hour after hour, longing and hoping to see her master. For hours together, too, she would sit on the stone at the four cross-roads, in sunshine or snow, wind or rain, with the tears coursing down her cheeks, and such a pain at her heart, that she hardly knew how to endure it.

He never came, though. To all appearances he had entirely forgotten poor, faulty Cherry, and by and by she died, unable to bear the loneliness any longer.

THE FAIRIES ON THE GUMP.

Down by St. Just, not far from Cape Cornwall and the sea, is a small hill,—or a very large mound would, perhaps, be the truer description,— called 'The Gump,' where the Small People used to hold their revels, and where our grandfathers and grandmothers used to be allowed to stand and look on and listen.

In those good old times fairies and ordinary people were all good friends together, and it is because they were all such friends and trusted one another so, that our grandfathers and grandmothers were able to tell their grandchildren so many tales about fairies, and piskies, and buccas, and all the rest of the Little People.

People believed in the Fairies in those days, so the Fairies in return often helped the people, and did them all sorts of kindnesses. Indeed, they would do so now if folks had not grown so learned and disbelieving. It seems strange that because they have got more knowledge of some matters, they should have grown more ignorant of others, and declare that there never were such things as Fairies, just because they have neither the eyes nor the minds to see them!

Of course, no one could expect the sensitive little creatures to appear when they are sneered at and scoffed at. All the same, though, they are as much about us as ever they were, and if you or I, who do believe in the Little People, were to go to the Gump on the right nights at the right hour, we should see them feasting and dancing and holding their revels just as of old. If, though, you do go, you must be very careful to keep at a distance, and not to trespass on their fairy ground, for that is a great offence, and woe be to you if you offend them!

There was, once upon a time, a grasping, mean old fellow who did so, and pretty well he was punished for his daring. It is his story I am going to tell you, but I will not tell you his name, for that would be unpleasant for his descendants, but I will tell you this much,—he was a St. Just man, and no credit to the place either, I am sure.

Well, this old man used to listen to the tales the people told of the Fairies and their riches, and their wonderful treasures, until he could scarcely bear to hear any more, he longed so to have some of those riches for himself; and at last his covetousness grew so great, he said to himself he must and would have some, or he should die of vexation.

So one night, when the Harvest Moon was at the full, he started off alone, and very stealthily, to walk to the Gump, for he did not want his neighbours to know anything at all about his plans. He was very nervous, for it is a very desolate spot, but his greed was greater than his fear, and he made himself go forward, though he longed all the time to turn tail and hurry home to the safe shelter of his house and his bed.

When he was still at some distance from the enchanted spot, strains of the most exquisite music anyone could possibly imagine reached his ear, and as he stood listening it seemed to come nearer and nearer until, at last, it was close about him. The most wonderful part, though, of it all was that there was nothing to be seen, no person, no bird, not an animal even. The empty moor stretched away on every side, the Gump lay bare and desolate before him. The only living being on it that night was himself.

The music, indeed, seemed to come from under the ground, and such strange music it was, too, so gentle, so touching, it made the old miser weep, in spite of himself, and then, even while the tears were still running down his cheeks, he was forced to laugh quite merrily, and even to dance, though he certainly did not want to do either. After that it was not surprising that he found himself marching along, step and step, keeping time with the music as it played, first slowly and with stately tread, then fast and lively.

All the time, though, that he was laughing and weeping, marching or dancing, his wicked mind was full of thoughts as to how he should get at the fairy treasure.

At last, when he got close to the Gump, the music ceased, and suddenly, with a loud crashing noise which nearly scared the old man out of his senses, the whole hill seemed to open as if by magic, and in one instant every spot was lighted up. Thousands of little lights of all colours gleamed everywhere, silver stars twinkled and sparkled on every furze-bush, tiny lamps hung from every blade of grass. It was a more lovely sight than one ever sees nowadays, more lovely than any pantomime one has ever seen or ever will see. Then, out from the open hill marched troops of little Spriggans.

Spriggans, you must know, are the Small People who live in rocks and stones, and cromlechs, the most mischievous, thievish little creatures that ever lived, and woe betide anyone who meddles with their dwelling-places.

Well, first came all those Spriggans, then a large band of musicians followed by troops of soldiers, each troop carrying a beautiful banner, which waved and streamed out as though a brisk breeze were blowing, whereas in reality there was not a breath of wind stirring.

These hosts of Little People quickly took up their places in perfect order all about the Gump, and, though they appeared quite unconscious of his presence, a great number formed a ring all round the old man. He was greatly amazed, but, "Never mind," he thought, "they are such little whipper-snappers I can easily squash them with my foot if they try on any May-games with me."

As soon as the musicians, the Spriggans, and the soldiers had arranged themselves, out came a lot of servants carrying most lovely gold and silver vessels, goblets, too, cut out of single rubies, and diamonds, and emeralds, and every kind of precious stone. Then came others bearing rich meats and pastry, luscious fruits and preserves, everything, in fact, that one could think of that was dainty and appetizing. Each servant placed his burden on the tables in its proper place, then silently retired.

Can you not imagine how the glorious scene dazzled the old man, and how his eyes glistened, and his fingers itched to grab at some of the wonderful things and carry them off? He knew that even one only of those flashing goblets would make him rich for ever.

He was just thinking that nowhere in the world could there be a more beautiful sight, when, lo and behold! the illumination became twenty times as brilliant, and out of the hill came thousands and thousands of exquisitely dressed ladies and gentlemen, all in rows, each gentleman leading a lady, and all marching in perfect time and order.

They came in companies of a thousand each, and each company was differently attired. In the first the gentlemen were all dressed in yellow satin covered with copper-coloured spangles, on their heads they wore copper-coloured helmets with waving, yellow plumes, and on their feet yellow shoes with copper heels. The flashing of the copper in the moonlight was almost blinding. Their companions all were dressed alike in white satin gowns edged with large turquoises, and on their tiny feet pale blue shoes with buckles formed of one large turquoise set in pearls.

The gentlemen conducted the ladies to their places on the Gump, and with a courtly bow left them, themselves retiring to a little distance. The next troop then came up, in this the gentlemen were all attired in black, trimmed with silver, silver helmets with black plumes, black stockings and silver shoes. Their ladies were dressed in pink embroidered in gold, with waving pink plumes in their hair, and golden buckles on their pink shoes. In the next troop the men were dressed in blue and white, the ladies in green, with diamonds all around the hem of the gown, diamonds flashing in their hair, and hanging in long ropes from their necks; on their green shoes single diamonds blazed and flashed.

So they came, troop after troop, more than I can describe, or you could remember, only I must tell you that the last of all were the most lovely. The ladies, all of whom had dark hair, were clad in white velvet lined with the palest violet silk, while round the hems of the skirts and on the bodices were bands of soft white swansdown. Swansdown also edged the little violet cloaks which hung from their shoulders. I cannot describe to you how beautiful they looked, with their rosy, smiling faces, and long black curls. On their heads they wore little silver crowns set with amethysts, amethysts, too, sparkled on their necks and over their gowns. In their hands they carried long trails of the lovely blossom of the wistaria. Their companions were clad in white and green, and in their left hands they carried silver rods with emerald stars at the top.

It really seemed at one time as though the troops of Little People would never cease pouring out of the hill. They did so at last, though, and as soon as all were in their places the music suddenly changed, and became more exquisite than ever.

The old man by this time seemed able to see more clearly, and hear more distinctly, and his sense of smell grew keener. Never were such flashing gems as here, never had any flowers such scents as these that were here.

There were now thousands of little ladies gathered on the Gump, and these all broke out into song at the same instant, such beautiful singing, too, so sweet and delicate. The words were in an unknown tongue, but the song was evidently about some great personages who were about to emerge from the amazing hill, for again it opened, and again poured forth a crowd of Small People.

First of all came a bevy of little girls in white gauze, scattering flowers, which, as soon as they touched the ground, sprang up into full life and threw out leaves and more flowers, full of exquisite scents; then came a number of boys playing on shells as though they were harps, and making ravishing music, while after them came hundreds and hundreds of little men clad in green and gold, followed by a perfect forest of banners spreading and waving on the air.

Then last, but more beautiful than all that had gone before, was carried a raised platform covered with silk embroidered with real gold, and edged with crystals, and on the platform were seated a prince and princess of such surpassing loveliness that no words can be found to describe them. They were dressed in the richest velvet, and covered with precious stones which blazed and sparkled in the myriad lights until the eye could scarce bear to look at them.

Over her lovely robe the princess's hair flowed down to the floor, where it rested in great shining, golden waves. In her hand she held a golden sceptre, on the top of which blazed a diamond as large as a walnut, while the prince carried one with a sapphire of equal size. After a deal of marching backwards and forwards, the platform was placed on the highest point of the Gump, which was now a hill of flowers, and every fairy walked up and bowed, said something to the prince and princess, and passed on to a seat at the tables. And the marvel was that though there were so many fairies present, there was not the slightest confusion amongst them, not one person moved out of place at the wrong moment. All was as quiet and well-arranged as could possibly be.

At length all were seated, whereupon the prince gave a signal, on which a number of footmen came forward carrying a table laden with dainty food in solid gold dishes, and wines in goblets of precious stones which they placed on the platform before the prince and princess. As soon as the royal pair began to eat, all the hosts around them followed their example, and such a merry, jovial meal they had. The viands disappeared as fast as they could go, laughter and talk sounded on all sides, and never a sign did any of them give that they knew that a human being was watching them. If they knew it, they showed not the slightest concern.

"Ah!" thought the old miser to himself. "I can't get all I'd like to, but if I could reach up to the prince's table I could get enough at one grab to set me up for life, and make me the richest man in St. Just parish!"

Stooping down, he slowly and stealthily dragged himself nearer and nearer to the table. He felt quite sure that no one could see him. What he himself did not see was that hundreds of wicked little Spriggans had tied ropes on to him, and were holding fast to the ends. He crawled and crawled so slowly and carefully that it took him some time to get over the ground, but he managed it at last, and got quite close up to the lovely little pair. Once there he paused for a moment and looked back,—perhaps to see if the way was clear for him to run when he had done what he meant to do. He was rather startled to find that all was as dark as dark could be, and that he could see nothing at all behind him. However, he tried to cheer himself by thinking that it was only that his eyes were dazzled by looking at the bright lights so long. He was even more startled, though, when he turned round to the Gump again, to find that every eye of all those hundreds and thousands of fairies on the hill was looking straight into his eyes.

At first he was really frightened, but as they did nothing but look, he told himself that they could not really be gazing at him, and grew braver with the thought. Then slowly bringing up his hat, as a boy does to catch a butterfly, he was just going to bring it down on the silken platform and capture prince and princess, table, gold dishes and all, when hark! A shrill whistle sounded, the old man's hand, with the hat in it, was paralysed in the air, so that he could not move it backwards or forwards, and in an instant every light went out, and all was pitchy darkness.

There were a whir-r-r and a buzz, and a whir-r-r, as if a swarm of bees were flying by him, and the old man felt himself fastened so securely to the ground that, do what he would, he could not move an inch, and all the time he felt himself being pinched, and pricked, and tweaked from top to toe, so that not an inch of him was free from torment. He was lying on his back at the foot of the Gump, though how he got there he could never tell. His arms were stretched out and fastened down, so that he could not do anything to drive off his tormentors, his legs were so secured that he could not even relieve himself by kicking, and his tongue was tied with cords, so that he could not call out.

There he lay, no one knows how long, for to him it seemed hours, and no one else but the fairies knew anything about it. At last he felt a lot of little feet running over him, but whose they were he had no idea until something perched on his nose, and by the light of the moon he saw it was a Spriggan. His wicked old heart sank when he realized that he had got into their clutches, for all his life he had heard what wicked little creatures they were.

The little imp on his nose kicked and danced and stamped about in great delight at finding himself perched up so high. We all know how painful it is to have one's nose knocked, even ever so little, so you may imagine that the old miser did not enjoy himself at all. Master Spriggan did, though. He roared with laughter, as though he were having a huge joke, until at last, rising suddenly to his feet and standing on the tips of his tiny toes, he shouted sharply, "Away! away! I smell the day!" and to the old man's great relief off he flew in a great hurry, followed by all his mischievous little companions who had been playing games, and running races all over their victim's body.

Left at last to himself, the mortified old man lay for some time, thinking over all that had happened, trying to collect his senses, and wondering how he should manage to escape from his bonds, for he might lie there for a week without any human being coming near the place.

Till sunrise he lay there, trying to think of some plan, and then, what do you think he saw? Why, that he had not been tied down by ropes at all, but only by thousands of gossamer webs! And there they were now, all over him, with the dew on them sparkling like the diamonds that the princess had worn the night before. And those dewdrop diamonds were all the jewels he got for his night's work.

When he made this discovery he turned over and groaned and wept with rage and shame, and never, to his dying day, could he bear to look at sparkling gold or gems, for the mere sight of them made him feel quite ill.

At last, afraid lest he should be missed, and searchers be sent out to look for him, he got up, brushed off the dewy webs, and putting on his battered old hat, crept slowly home. He was wet through with dew, cold, full of rheumatism, and very ashamed of himself, and very good care he took to keep that night's experiences to himself. No one must know his shame.

Years after, though, when he had become a changed man, and repented of his former greediness, he let out the story bit by bit to be a lesson to others, until his friends and neighbours, who loved to listen to anything about fairies, had gathered it all as I have told it to you here. And you may be quite sure it is all true, for the old man was not clever enough to invent it.

THE FAIRY OINTMENT.

Now I will tell you a story of a very foolish woman, whose curiosity got the better of her, and of how she was punished.

The old woman's Christian name was Joan. I will not tell her surname, for it does not make any difference to the story, and there may be some of her descendants left who would not like it to be known. Joan was housekeeper to Squire Lovell. The name of his house shall be kept a secret too, but I will tell you this much, that he lived a few miles out of Penzance.

Now one Saturday afternoon it fell out that Joan wanted to go to Penzance Market to get herself a pair of shoes, and to buy some groceries and several Christmas things for the house, for it was Christmas Eve, and the Squire had a lot of folks coming to supper that very night. So, the weather being fine, Joan started off soon after her twelve o'clock dinner, to walk into Penzance to market. Having, though, a great fancy for company, and loving a little gossip, she thought she would step in on her way to see if her friend Betty Trenance was going to market too. It would be so nice to have each other's company on the way.

Now many persons in those parts told some very queer stories about Betty Trenance, and amongst themselves some called her a witch, and were afraid of her. Joan, though, argued that if she was a witch, there was all the more reason for keeping friendly with her. And if one did not offend Betty, she was always ready to give one a cup of tea, or do anything to oblige one.

Betty lived down at Lamorna Cove, which was a little way out of Joan's road, but she did not mind that if she could get Betty's company. She walked quickly, though, for the days were short, and she had a long way to go, and to be back in time to cook the Squire's supper. On her way she met two of Betty's elder children carrying baskets of fish on their backs, and down in the Cove she saw all the younger ones at play with the limpets and crabs in the rock-pools, and paddling about in the water. But she could not stay to watch them, for she had no time to spare, so she hurried on to the cottage.

When she got there, though, to her astonishment she found the front door was closed and fastened, not only latched either, but bolted! This was such an unusual thing in those parts, that Joan was quite startled. At first she thought something must really have gone amiss, then she comforted herself by deciding that Betty had already started for the market, and had locked the children out to keep them from ransacking the place. Just, though, as she had settled all this in her mind, and was about to turn away, the sound of voices reached her, and voices talking very earnestly, too.

Joan looked round her nervously, the voices sounded quite near to her, but there was no sight or sign of any living thing except some seagulls, and Betty's old black cat.

What did it all mean? Joan was frightened, but her curiosity made her stay and try to get to the bottom of the mystery. She stood quite still and listened very closely. Yes, there were the voices again, plainly enough, but where? She tiptoed close up to the door and placed her ear against the keyhole. This time she heard Tom Trenance's voice quite distinctly,—Tom was Betty's husband. He was talking very earnestly to someone too, more earnestly than she had ever heard him speak in her life before, but, try as she would, she could not make out to whom he was speaking, nor what he was saying.

This was more than inquisitive Joan could endure. She must know what was going on in that cottage, or she would know no peace day or night, for thinking about it. So she made up her mind to knock and knock until those inside were obliged to come to the door, but first of all she thought she would have a peep in through the finger-hole by the latch. So she stooped down and put her eye to the hole, and there she saw Tom sitting on the settle, and after all it was only Betty that he was talking to.

Betty was standing beside him with a little box in her hand, from which she took something that looked like ointment, which she smeared over her husband's eyes, and all the time she did it she seemed to be mumbling some verses or something that sounded like a charm. There seemed to be other voices as well, though, and to Joan's great annoyance she could not see from whence they came.

All this put old Joan in a fearful flutter. People had always told her that Betty was a witch, and that Tom had the power of the evil eye, and now she began to believe them. You would not have thought so to look at him, for though they were very piercing, they were handsome hazel eyes, clear and kind-looking,—unless he was angered, and then—

Completely mystified, and more inquisitive than ever, Joan went round to the window by the chimney, to see if from there she could hear what they were saying; but it was of no use. The door of the cottage was on the landward side, and the windows of the cottage were to seaward, and round the kitchen window was a great bush of honeysuckle and 'Traveller's Joy,' which prevented anyone's getting quite close, and what with the sound of the sea, the singing of the birds, and the shouting of the children below, one might as well have been a mile off, for all one could hear!

Back tiptoed Joan again, and sat down on the bench outside the house to think, but her curiosity would not let her keep still, so up she jumped again, and peeped through the door once more. This time she saw that Tom was standing up, preparing to come out; so not wanting to be caught prying, she tapped at the door, and lifting the latch at the same time, walked in as if she had but that moment arrived. She was so excited by what she was doing that she did not notice that the door opened quite easily now. She went in so quickly, too, that she was just in time to see Betty push something under the dried ferns at the back of the chimney.

After saying "good day," and hearing what she had come for, Tom went out, leaving them to make their plans by themselves, but Betty, though she seemed pleased to see her friend, could not be persuaded to go to market with her. She was very sorry, she said, but she was very bad, she had not been well for days, and she still had a good day's work to get through making ready for Christmas. She was not too busy, though, to make a cup of tea, and Joan must stay and have one with her, and away she bustled to the talfat,[1] where she had a special case of tea put away. This was Joan's opportunity, and she seized it. As soon as Betty's back was turned, she whipped the pot of ointment out from under the ferns, stuck her finger in it, and popped the pot back again, in no time. But no sooner had she touched her eye with the ointment than, oh! such a pain shot through it, she very nearly shrieked aloud. It was as though a red-hot knitting needle had been run right through her eyeball! And, oh, the smarting and the burning that followed! To prevent a sound escaping her she had to hug and squeeze herself with all her might, she dared not open her lips to speak, and the tears poured down her cheeks like rain.

It was lucky for her that Betty had some trouble in dragging the chest of tea from under the bed, for if she had come back quickly she could not have helped seeing what Joan had been doing. By the time she returned, though, the worst of the pain was over, and keeping up her hand to that side of her face, Joan managed to conceal the injured eye, and Betty was too busy with her fire and her kettle to be very observant.

"I'm glad you came in to have a cup with me, and drink my health, it being Christmas Eve and all," said Betty as they drew up to the table. Then, having drunk each other's health, they had a third cup to drink the health of the children, for, as Joan said, "there wasn't a healthier, handsomer family in the whole parish." Then they drank the health of the mermaids, for it is always wise to be civil to them, and after that Joan rose to go.

Before she could go, though, she felt she must manage to open her injured eye, which still watered and smarted a good deal. So she rubbed it and blinked and winked until at last she managed to part the lids,—when, lo and behold! to her amazement and alarm she saw that the house, which she had thought empty save for herself and Betty, was simply thronged with Little People!

There was not a spot that was free of them! They were climbing up the dressers, hanging on to the beams, swinging on the fishing nets, hanging across them, playing pranks on the clock, on the table, and the mantelpiece, sliding down the saucepan handles, riding races on mice,— they were everywhere, in fact, and up to every kind of game.

They were all very beautifully dressed. Most of the little men wore green velvet, trimmed with scarlet, and their long green caps, which most of them were waving frantically, had long scarlet feathers in them. They all wore little red boots, too, and large silver spurs,—at least, large for fairies.

The ladies were very consequential little people indeed, and swept about in their long-trained gowns as though they were Court ladies at a Drawing-room. On their little shoes they had diamond buckles, and their great steeple-crowned hats were garlanded with beautiful flowers. Such flowers as are seldom seen on Christmas Eve, but the Little People have gardens under the sea where the flowers bloom in wonderful beauty all the year round. Fishermen see them sometimes on moonlight nights, when the water is clear and the wind calm, and if they listen closely they can hear exquisite fairy music floating across the waters from bay to bay.

Back in the corner by Betty's wood heap were a lot of Spriggans, poor depressed little creatures, dirty and sullen-looking. They were not lively like the others, for you know they have to guard the Fairy treasures all the year round, and they get no fun at all, as other fairies do. So they are naturally not very lively.

While Joan was standing gazing, open-mouthed, bewildered by what she saw, strains of the most beautiful music reached her ears, and gradually a change began to come over the whole house. It was no wonder that she thought her head was turned! The music came nearer and nearer, and mingling with it was the tramp of hundreds of little feet; at last it came quite close, and through the window marched a regiment of robins as unconcernedly as a regiment of soldiers entering their barracks. Quite gravely they stepped down from the window, marched across the room, and flew up to the beam, where they perched themselves in perfect order, and began to sing as hard as they possibly could. In a moment or two they were followed through the window by a regiment of wrens, and then by a regiment of Little People, all playing on every kind of musical instrument ever invented, and on a number made out of reeds, and shells, such as had never been seen before or since.

Stepping down gracefully from the window to the floor, the band, followed by numbers of little ladies and gentlemen, carrying branches of herbs and flowers, marched with stately tread past old Betty Trenance, bowed to her in a most respectful manner in passing, then arranged themselves in perfect order behind her. Last of all came another troop of fairies, and these took the herbs and flowers brought by the little ladies and gentlemen and placed them in Betty's apron.

"These are what she makes her salves and ointments of," thought Joan to herself; "no wonder she is thought so clever."

This done, all the other fairies who had been playing about the house came down to the floor and joined the new-comers. Such a crowd never was seen! No sooner had the flowers and herbs been heaped in Betty's lap than another troop of fairies came forward with fox-glove bells full of dyes, which they poured over Betty's dress, when in a moment her russet gown was changed to the softest white velvet, her apron to the filmiest lace, edged all round with a delicate fringe of harebells and snowdrops. Other fairies outlined the quilted 'diamonds' of her petticoat with silver cord.

When her dress had been transformed in this way, all the troop of Little People came forward with dainty bunches of flowers to complete her toilet, sweet wild flowers they were, delicate speedwells and forget-me-nots with their fresh green, and their innocent blue eyes; the warm scarlet pimpernel, violets, snowdrops, heather bells, and ladies' white petticoats. Some of each and every kind of flower we find in the lanes and hedges. The little ladies stitched a small nosegay in each 'diamond' of Betty's petticoat, and every nosegay was different. The tiniest flowers of all they laid on sprays of feathery moss, others had background of graceful ferns, or delicate grass. Around the hem of the skirt were sprays of pink and white dog-roses, while the bodice was wreathed with tiny pink and white convolvulus. Sparkling at Betty's throat were such brilliant jewels that Joan had to look away, her eyes were so dazzled.

The strangest part of all this was that Betty did not seem in the least surprised at what was going on, and was apparently quite unaware that Joan was watching her.

As soon as the gown was completed, another group of the clever little creatures clambered up to the top of the high-backed chair in which Betty was seated, and began to arrange her hair. Some had quaint little pots in their hands from which they poured delicate perfumes over Betty's head,— Joan picked up one of the pots, which they threw aside when empty, and found to her astonishment that it was only a poppy head. Then they carefully arranged every curl and wave of

Betty's hair, until she looked as beautiful as a queen, and as dignified and stately, too; for Betty, though a mischievous witch, was not at all like our ideas of one. She was as clean as a new pin, and as neat and tidy as anyone could be. Her features were unusually handsome, and her thick dark hair, which reached the ground when she sat down, was full of the prettiest curls and waves.

As soon as the last curl was arranged, and her tire-maidens satisfied, they placed a spray of jessamine amongst her tresses, and jumped down, their task completed.

All this time the music was playing the most bewitching melodies.

Very soon after this Joan began to have a feeling that Betty wished her gone. The Little People, too, were making signs that she could not fail to understand, and such hideous grimaces at her, too, that made her long to box their ears. Of course, neither Betty nor the fairies knew that she had used the Fairy Ointment, and could see them, and to save herself from being found out, she bade her friend 'goodbye' with all speed.

When Joan got outside, though, she could not resist one more sly peep in, just to make sure she had not been dreaming. So down went her eye to the finger-hole again, but all she saw was the kitchen, with its sanded floor and bright turf fire, the key-beam with the nets hanging across it, and Betty stitching away as fast as her fingers could fly.

"This is the most extraordinary thing I ever heard tell of," said Joan to herself. "I'll have another look."

Down went her eye again, but the right one this time, and, lo and behold! there was the kitchen turned into a splendid banqueting hall, hung around with tapestry representing everything that had ever happened in the world. The talfat-rail was turned into a balcony hung with pale blue satin, where sat a number of little ladies and gentlemen watching the dancing which was going on below. The costumes of all were magnificent, the cottage was as beautiful as a bit of Fairyland, and seated on a golden chair of state under a velvet canopy was Betty Trenance looking as royal as a queen.

Betty, though, seemed to be keeping a sharp eye on the door, and as she had a crowd of wicked little piskies about her, Joan thought it wise to get away to safer quarters. So off she hurried, but as she went she met numbers of fairies all hurrying away to Betty's cottage, while from the rocks below came the doleful wail of the mermaids, and all was so uncanny Joan was glad to hurry along as fast as she knew how. She was really scared by this time, and the light was growing dim, for it was already past three o'clock.

Once arrived at Penzance, Joan did her marketing quickly, but by the time she had finished she was very tired and very hungry, for she had had nothing to eat since twelve o'clock dinner, and had been trudging about for hours. So, having a piece of saffron cake in her basket, she turned into an inn in Market Jew Street, to get something to drink with it, and a place to sit down for a while to rest.

When she got there she found the house so crowded that she had to sit on a bench outside, and here she met a lot of friends, and had a thorough good gossip. They drank each other's health too, and passed the compliments of the season, until Joan remembered all of a sudden that she ought to have been on her way home by that time, for the Squire would be very angry if she were not there to see to things for the supper-party.

Up she jumped in a great flurry, and had said 'good-bye' all round when she suddenly remembered that she had not yet bought several of the things she had come to town on purpose to get. She was dreadfully vexed, but there was no time to stay and think about it, she had just to hurry back into the market and make her purchases as quickly as possible.

At last she had really bought everything, and was about to leave, when unfortunately some wonderful bargains caught her eye, and it did seem to her sinful to go away without taking a glance at them when she might never have such a chance again. So she lingered by the stalls, and wandered up and down having a good look at everything, when whom should she see doing the very same thing but Tom Trenance!

He did not see Joan, so she thought she would go up and speak to him, and ask if he was going home soon, for it would be nice to have his company on the way. He was so busy, though, darting about from stall to stall, that Joan could never get up to him. But she could see what he was doing, and the sight made Joan's blood boil with indignation! He was helping himself to everything that took his fancy! Yarn, stockings, boots, spoons, clothing, until the wonder was that he could manage to stow the things away.

The oddest part of all, though, was that nobody seemed to see him. Joan looked again and again to make sure she was not dreaming, but no, he was there right enough, and pocketing things as fast as he could, right under the stall-keepers' very noses, and they paying no heed whatever to him!

Joan could bear it no longer! She could not stand by and see such wickedness going on; it made her blood boil with indignation. So over she bustled and touched him on the arm.

"Tom Trenance," she cried, "I'm downright ashamed of 'ee! I wonder you ain't above carrying on such dishonest ways, and you with children to set an example to! I didn't think you capable of such wickedness."

Tom for a minute looked, and was too much taken aback to speak. But he quickly recovered himself. "Why, Joan," he said, taking no notice of her accusations, "I take it very kind and neighbourly of 'ee to come up and speak. What sharp eyes you've got! Now which of them did you 'appen to catch sight of me with?"

"Which? Why, both, of course," cried Joan, but she put up her hand first over one and then over the other, and found she could only see Tom with the right one. "Why, no, I can't see 'ee with both," she cried in astonishment. "The left one don't seem to be a bit of good!"

"The right one is it?" said Tom, and his look went through her like a gimlet. Then, pointing his finger at it, he muttered:—

And at that very moment a sharp pain shot through her right eye. It was so sharp that she screamed aloud, and from that moment she never could see with it again.

Yelling, and pressing her fist into her throbbing eyeball, she rushed hither and thither, calling to people to come and help her, and to go and catch Tom Trenance, all in one breath; but as they could not see Tom,—nor could she, either, now,—they unkindly said the poor soul was crazy, which, of course, was most unjust and cruel of them, and shows what mistakes people can make.

Of course, it was the Fairy Ointment on her eye which enabled her to see so much, and it was that same ointment which rendered Tom Trenance invisible to everyone but to her.

How poor Joan ever found her way back to Market Jew Street again she never could tell, but when she did arrive there she had, of course, to stay a little while and tell her sad story, so that it was really quite late and dark before she started for home; and then, what with the darkness and her blindness she could only crawl along. She groped her way painfully down Voundervoor and over the Green, stumbling over the ruts and sandy banks until she was very nearly driven crazy. Through only being able to see with her left eye, she kept bearing away to the left side of the road, and I cannot tell you how many times she fell into the ditch, marketing and all! And so afraid was she of falling into the sea, and so close did she keep to the other side of the road away from it, that at last she went right through the hedge and fell over into a place called 'Park-an-Shebbar!'

Luckily one of the farm-boys was in the field, and helped her up and picked up her parcels for her; then, seeing how bad she was, he took her into the house to rest and recover, for she seemed quite dazed by that time. There they gave her something to bring her round, and presently she began to feel better and able to go on again.

By this time she was very anxious to get home, so the lad helped her over the stream and set her on the right road once more. This time Joan stepped out briskly, for she was really very troubled about the Squire's supper, and all the people who were expected to it. If she did not get home soon, they would have arrived first, and, oh, how angry the Squire would be!

By the time, though, that she got to the top of Paul Hill, she was so tired she felt she could not go another step without a rest, so, though she could badly spare the time, she dropped with a sigh of relief on to a soft green spot, when, oh! what a shriek she gave! for the soft green spot was a duck-pond covered with duck-weed! How she got out of the pond she could never tell, but she did and crept over to the other side of the road, where she fell back on the hedge quite exhausted.

"Oh dear, oh dear!" she moaned, "I'm nearly dead. Oh, if only I'd got our old Dumpling here to give me a lift; or any other quiet old horse I'd be thankful for. I shall never reach home to-night on my two feet, I'm sure, they are ready to drop off already!"

Barely had she uttered her wish when there by the roadside stood an old white horse, cropping quietly away at the brambles and dead ferns. How he came there I can't tell you. Whether he had been there all the time without her seeing him, or whether he came by magic, no one can say, but there he was.

Many persons in Dame Joan's place would have been afraid to mount him, fearing witchcraft, or fairies' pranks, but Joan was too tired to have many scruples. So up she got and untied his feet, for he was hobbled, put the rope round his head, and then managed somehow to clamber up on his back, basket and all. It was hard work, but she got settled after a bit, then picking up the rope, called to him to start.

"Gee wug! gee wo!" she called, "get up, you lazy old faggot!" and she hammered away at his side with her heels with all her might—and her shoes were none of the daintiest! but in spite of her coaxings and her threats, her kicks and her thumps, the old horse did not move an inch.

"Come up, can't you! Gee wug, come here!" She beat him and kicked him again until she was really too tired to move hand or foot; then, when she had given up in despair, the tiresome creature made a start. But such a start! he went at a slow snail's pace, and try as Joan would she could not make him go faster.

At last, though, when she reached the top of a hill, there came from the valley below the cry of hounds, devil's hounds they must have been, for no others would be out at that time of night. As soon as the sounds reached the old horse's ears, he pricked them up, whinnied loudly, and with a toss of his head and a fling of his tail started away like any young colt.

Away, away, uphill and downhill they tore as fast as the wind. Joan clung to the horse's mane with both hands, and yelled and yelled to him to stop. She might as well, though, have held her breath. All her marketing flew out of her basket, her precious beaver hat was carried away, her shawl was whisked off her back! On and on the old horse tore, jumping over everything that came in his way, until Joan was nearly flung from his back. Presently, too, to her horror she saw that the creature was growing bigger and bigger, and higher and higher; soon he shot up above the trees, then he was as high as the church tower. Poor Joan, perched on his back, grew sick, giddy, and terrified. She was afraid now to slip off lest she should be dashed to pieces, and was afraid to stay there lest she should fall off.

For miles and miles they travelled like this, until at last they came to Toldave Moor, on the further side of which there was, Joan knew, a deep black pool, and for this pool, to Joan's horror, the monster galloped straight!

"If I don't slip off now, I shall surely be drowned outright!" thought poor Joan, for the pond was deep, she felt her powers were failing her; her hands were numb, her limbs cramped. She knew she could not swim. "Better a dry death than a wet one, it will save my clothes, anyway!" So, letting go her hold of the creature's mane, she was about to let herself slide down, when the wind caught her and carried her right off the horse's back. They were going at a terrific rate, and the wind was very keen on the moor; it lifted her right up in the air, high above the horse, and then, just as she thought she was going to disappear through the clouds, she was dropped plump into the rushes by the edge of the very pool itself.

At the same moment the air became filled with the most awful clamour, such yells and cries, and terrible laughter as no living being had ever heard before. Poor old Joan thought her last hour had really come, and gave herself up for lost, for when she looked round she saw the fearful great creature she had been riding, disappearing in the distance in flames of fire, and tearing after it, helter-skelter, pell-mell, was a horrible crew of men and dogs and horses. Two or three hundred of them there must have been, and not one of the lot had a head on his shoulders.

Joan would have screamed, too, if she had not been stricken dumb with fright; so, very nearly scared to death, trembling with cold and fear, there she lay until they had disappeared.

How she scrambled out of her soft, damp resting-place she could never tell, but she did, somehow, and got as far as Trove Bottom, though without any shoes, for they had come off in the ditch. Her shawl was gone, too, and all her marketing, and, worst of all, her precious broad-brimmed beaver hat.

There was a linhay down at the Bottom, where Squire Lovell kept a lot of sheep, and into that Joan crept, and lay down, and from sheer exhaustion fell asleep and slept till morning. How much longer she would have slept no one knows, but on Sunday mornings it was the Squire's habit to go down and look over his sheep, and on this Sunday, though it was Christmas Day, he visited them as usual.

His entrance with his boys and his dogs and his flashing lantern woke old Joan with a start, and so certain was she that they were the horse, and the huntsmen, and their hounds come again, that she sprang up in a frenzy of terror. "Get out, get out!" she cried, "let a poor old woman be!" But instead of the hollow laugh of the huntsmen, it was the Squire's voice that answered her.

"Why, here's our poor old lost Joan!" he cried, amazed, "and frightened out of her wits, seemingly! Why, Joan," he said, "whatever have you been spending the night out here for? We've been scouring the country for you, for hours!"

"Oh, Master!" she cried, almost in tears as she dropped trembling at his feet, "for the sake of all the years I've served 'ee from your cradle up, do 'ee let me die in peace, and bury me decent!" and then, her tongue once set going, she poured out all the long tale of the dreadful things that had happened to her since she set out for Penzance Market.

How long she would have talked no one knows, but the Squire sent for his men, and between them they carried her home, and warmed and fed and comforted her, for she was black and blue, wet to the skin, and half frozen. However, with all their care she soon recovered, and when she was dry, and warm, and rested she poured out all her adventures and disasters.

To her astonishment, though, and anger and pain, they refused to believe a word of it. They did not pity her a bit; they even laughed at her. Indeed, they tried to make her believe that the enchanted steed was only the miller's old white horse, that the demon huntsman and his hounds were no more nor less than her own son John riding across the moor with the dogs, in search of her, that her lost eye must have been scratched out by a 'fuz'-bush; and so they went on pooh-poohing the whole of her story,— which was very nearly the most aggravating thing of all she had had to bear.

One thing, though, Joan had not told them, and that was about her stealing the Fairy Ointment, or they would have known that she had been pisky-led that night, by order of the Fairies, as a punishment, and would one and all have agreed that she richly deserved it.

[1] A 'talfat' is a raised floor at one end of a cottage, on which a bed is placed. Sometimes it is divided off by a wooden partition, but more often there is only a bar, to prevent the sleeper falling out of bed.

THE EXCITING ADVENTURE OF JOHN STURTRIDGE.

One of the greatest feast-days in Cornwall, and the most looked forward to, is St. Picrons' Day, which falls just before Christmas. It is the special day of the tinners and streamers, their greatest holiday in the year, and on it they have a great merry-making. Picrons was the discoverer of tin in Cornwall, so they say, so, of course, it is the bounden duty of those who earn their living by it, to keep up his day with rejoicings.

It is not of St. Picrons, though, that I am going to tell you, but of John Sturtridge, a streamer, and what befell him one year when he had been keeping up St. Picrons' Day.

He had been up to the 'Rising Sun' to the great supper that was always held there, and to the merry-making after it, and had enjoyed himself mightily. Enjoyed himself so much, in fact, that he did not greatly relish having to turn out, when both were ended, and face a long walk home.

It was a bitterly cold night, and the road was a lonely one, all across Tregarden Downs. However, it had to be faced, and nothing was gained by putting it off, so John started, and at first he got along pretty well. True, he found the roads very puzzling, and difficult to follow, but that may have been the fault of the moonlight, or the will-o'-the-wisps. Anyhow, if he did not get on very rapidly, he got on somehow, and presently reached the Downs.

Now Tregarden Downs is a horribly wild, uncanny stretch of country, a place where no one chooses to walk alone after nightfall, and, though John was in a cheerful mood, and did not feel at all frightened, he quickened his steps, and pulled hot-foot for home and bed. He kept a sharp eye on the cart-tracks, too, for he had no fancy for going astray here as he had done in the lanes. Whether, though, he did go a little astray or not, no one can say, but all of a sudden what should he come upon right across his path, but a host of piskies playing all sorts of games and high jinks under the shelter of a great granite boulder.

Whatever John's feelings may have been at the sight of them, the piskies were not troubled by the sight of John. They were not in the least alarmed, the daring little imps. They only burst into roars of wicked laughter, which pretty nearly scared the wits out of poor John, and made him take to his heels and run for his life! If only he could get off the Downs, he thought, he would be safe enough, but the Downs, of which he knew every yard, seemed to-night to stretch for miles and miles, and, try as he would, he could not find his way off them. He wandered round and round, and up and down, and to and fro, until at last he was obliged to admit to himself that he did not know in the least where he was, for he could not find a single landmark to guide him.

It is a very unpleasant thing to lose yourself on a big lonely Down, on a bleak winter's night, but it is ten times more unpleasant when you are pursued all the way by scores of mischievous little sprites, who shriek with laughter at you all the time, and from sheer wickedness delight in leading you into all the marshy places, the prickily 'fuz'-bushes, and rough boulders they can find, and nearly die of laughter when you prick or bump yourself, or get stuck in the mud.

John was thoroughly frightened, and thoroughly out of temper, and was meditating how he could punish his little tormentors, when suddenly from all sides rose a shrill cry. "Ho and away for Par Beach! Ho and away for Par Beach! Ho and away for Par Beach!"

Hardly knowing what he was doing John shouted, too. "Ho and away for Par Beach!" he yelled at the top of his voice, and almost before he had said the words he was caught high up in the air, and in another minute found himself on the great stretch of sands at Par. As soon as they had recovered their breath the piskies all formed up in rings and began to dance as fast as their little feet could move, and John with them.

"Ho and away for Squire Tremaine's cellar!" The shrill cry rang out again, even as they danced. John again repeated the cry, and in a flash found himself in the cellars at Heligan,—Squire Tremaine's place,—with his mischievous little companions swarming all over them. John felt no fear of them now. He joined them in all their pranks, and had a good time running from cask to cask, and bottle to bottle, opening everything and tasting the contents of most.

John at last became so confused he could not remember who he was or where he was; in fact, he was so confused and so sleepy that when the piskies called out, "Ho and away for Par Beach!" try as he would he could not speak, so the piskies flew off, and John was left behind alone.

John did not mind it in the least, at first, for it was much more pleasant in the shelter of the cellar, with plenty of wine to warm him, than it would be out on the desolate sands at Par, where the wind blows keenly enough to take one's ears off. John did mind it, though, the next morning, when the butler came and discovered him. He was groping his way between two rows of casks, trying to find his way to Luxulyan, he explained to the butler, but the butler, instead of putting him in the right road, led him at once to Squire Tremaine's study, where John told the wonderful story of his adventures.

Strangely enough, though, neither the Squire nor anyone else would believe a word of them, and without any consideration for poor John's feelings, they popped him into Bodmin Jail almost as quickly as the piskies and he had popped into the cellar. And worse still, before much time had elapsed, they tried him, convicted him, and sentenced him to be hanged.

Poor John! Here was a dreadful state of affairs, and all brought on an innocent man by those wicked piskies! There was no escape either, or hope of reprieve, for people were not so tender-hearted in those days as in these, and a man was not only sentenced to death for a trifle, but no one ever took any trouble to get him off.

Well, the fatal day came, and John was brought to the gallows, where a large crowd was gathered to see the execution; and there stood John, with the clergyman imploring him to confess, and free his mind of a load of falsehood; and the hangman waiting with the noose in his hand, waiting to slip it over poor John's head, when suddenly a beautiful little lady, dressed in white and silver, appeared in the midst of the crowd gathered at the gallows-foot.

No one saw her come, no one knew how she got there; but without a word from her, not knowing, indeed, why they did so, every man, woman, and child stood back and left a clear pathway for her right up to the scaffold.

There she paused, and stood, with her eyes fixed on the prisoner, who, however, did not see her, for he was too frightened to notice anything that was going on around him—until, "Ho and away for France!" rang out a sweet voice, which John recognized in a moment. With the sound of it his poor dazed senses returned, and the spirit to seize the chance of escape offered him.

"Ho and away for France!" he yelled. There was no danger of his not being able to shout this time! And then, before anyone there could collect his senses, the officers of justice saw their prisoner whisked away from out of their very grasp, and John was in France long before the executioner and the chaplain, the jailers and the crowd, had ceased gaping stupidly at each other.

THE TRUE STORY OF ANNE AND THE FAIRIES.

More than two hundred years ago there lived in the parish of St. Teath, a poor labouring man called Jefferies, and this man had one daughter, called Anne. Anne was a sweetly pretty girl, and a very intelligent one, too; but she was a terrible hoyden. She shocked all the old ladies in the village, and all the prim people, dreadfully, and instead of being ashamed, she seemed to glory in it.

Everyone wondered how she came to have such a spirit, and whom she took after, for her mother was as quiet and meek a little woman as ever was born, and always had been; while her father was a stern, silent man, who looked upon his flighty daughter as a thorn in his side, a cross laid upon him for his good. But the fact remains that Anne was the most daring of all the young people in the parish, doing things that even the boys were afraid to do, for she had no fear, nothing awed her, and there was nothing she would not attempt.

In those days the fairies and piskies, witches and goblins of all sorts were all over the land, and everyone knew it, and was more or less in awe of them. The young people appealed to the fairies for everything, to be helped in their work, to get love-draughts, to be made beautiful, and to know their fortunes. At the same time they all, except Anne, would have been scared to death if they had caught sight of one. Anne, indeed, often boldly declared that she longed to see them, and would love to have a talk with them; and she made up her mind that she would, too, and when once Anne had got an idea into her head, she generally managed to carry it out.

So, without saying anything to anyone, she went out every evening as soon as the sun was gone down, and wandered about looking into the fox-glove bells, and under the ferns, examining the Fairy Rings and every other likely spot, singing:—

For though she had got a very good and true sweetheart, named Tom, she had a great fancy for a fairy one. Perhaps she was thinking of the lovely presents that people said the fairies gave, or perhaps she thought that she would like to live in a palace, and be dressed in silks and velvet, none of which things could poor Tom give her, of course.

On moonlight nights Anne crept away by herself to the banks of the stream which ran through the valley, and here, walking against the current, she would sing:—

She sang it wistfully enough to touch the heart of any fairy, but though she went on for a long time repeating all the charms she knew, and trying, by every means she could think of, to please the Little People, and though she often nearly put her hand on one during her searches, the Little People never showed themselves to her.

They noticed her, though, and were only biding their time.

One beautiful warm summer's day, Anne, having finished her housework early, took her knitting and went and sat in an arbour at the foot of the garden, for she never could bear to be cooped up indoors if she could possibly get out. She had not been sitting there very long when she heard a rustling amongst the bushes, but she took no notice of it, for she felt it was sure to be her lover, coming to have a talk with her; and now that she was so possessed with the thought of a fairy lover, she had ceased to care for poor Tom, and was extremely cool and off-hand with him.

So, at the sound of the rustling, even when it was repeated, she did not even raise her eyes from her knitting, or turn her head.

Presently, though, the bushes were rustled more violently, and then someone gave a little laugh. Anne moved this time, for the laugh was certainly not Tom's laugh.

A lane ran along at the back of the arbour, a lane which one had to pass down to get to the garden gate, and it was from here that the laugh came. Anne peeped carefully out through the trellis-work and bushes to try to see who it was who was laughing at her, but not a sign of any living being could she see. She felt annoyed, for it is extremely unpleasant to feel that someone is looking at you through a peep-hole, and making game of you.

Anne grew so vexed she could not keep her vexation to herself. "Well," she said aloud, feeling sure it was Tom who was trying to tease her, "you may stay there till the moss grows over you, before ever I'll come out to you."

A burst of laughter, peculiarly sweet and ringing, greeted her words. "Oh," she thought to herself, "whoever can it be? I'm certain sure Tom could never laugh like that. Who can it be, I wonder?"

She felt really nervous now, for there was something unnatural about it all, but she tried to reassure herself by thinking that nothing could happen to her in broad daylight such as it was then. Besides which, she did not know of anyone who wished to harm her, for she was a favourite with everyone in the village. She waited anxiously, though, to see what would happen next.

She went on with her knitting, seemingly paying no heed to anything, but her ears were strained to catch the least sound, and when, after a little while, the garden gate was softly opened and closed again, she heard it distinctly, and glancing up to see who was coming, she saw to her astonishment, not Tom, or anyone else she knew, but six little pisky gentlemen, handsome little creatures, with pleasant smiles and brilliantly shining eyes.

To her astonishment they did not seem at all disturbed at seeing her, but came up and ranged themselves in a row before her and bowed to the ground. They were all dressed alike in green knickerbockers and tunics, edged with scarlet, and tiny green caps, and one, the handsomest of the lot, had a beautiful red waving feather at one side of his. They stood and looked at Anne and smiled, and Anne, not at all frightened now, but pleased, smiled back at them. Then he with the red feather stepped in front of the others, and bowing to her in the most courtly manner, addressed her with a charming friendliness which set her at ease at once.

Whether this strange little gentleman was really attracted by her charms, or whether he acted in the same way to every pretty girl he met, one cannot say, but he certainly looked at Anne very affectionately and admiringly, and poor Anne's heart was captured at once. She was certain there never had been such a charming little gentleman before, nor ever could be again, nor one with such good taste.

Stooping down she held out her hand, whereupon the little gentleman stepped into it, and Anne lifted him to her lap. From her lap he soon climbed to her shoulder, and then he kissed her, and not only kissed her once, but many times, and Anne thought him more charming than ever. Presently he called his companions, and they climbed up and kissed Anne, too, and patted her rosy cheeks, and smoothed her hair. But while one of them was patting her cheek, he ran his finger across her eyes, and Anne gave a terrible scream, for with his touch she felt as though a needle had been run through her eyeballs, and when she tried to open them again she found she was blind.

At the same moment she felt herself caught up in the air, and for what seemed to her a very long time she was carried through it at a tremendous rate. At last they came to a stop, whereupon one of the Little Men said something which Anne could not understand, and, behold, her eyesight at once came back!

And now, indeed, she had something to use it on, for she found herself in what seemed to be a perfectly gorgeous palace, or rather two or three palaces joined together, all built of gold and silver, with arches and pillars of crystal, large halls with walls of burnished copper, and beautiful rooms inlaid with precious marbles. Outside was a perfect paradise of a garden, filled with lovely flowers, and trees laden with fruit or blossom. Birds were singing everywhere, such rare birds, too! Some were all blue and gold, others a bright scarlet, then again others shone like silver or steel. There were large lakes full of gold and silver fish, and marble fountains throwing jets of water high into the air. Here and there were dainty bowers covered with roses, and filled within with soft moss carpets and luxurious couches. Walking about everywhere in this lovely place were scores of little ladies and gentlemen, dressed in rich silks and velvets, and with precious stones sparkling and flashing from their fingers, their hair, their shoes, indeed they seemed to sparkle all over, like flowers covered with dewdrops. Some strolled along the walks, others reclined in the bowers, some floated in little scarlet or ivory boats on the lakes, others sat under the blossoming trees. There seemed, indeed, no end to them, and to Anne's great astonishment, neither they nor her six companions seemed small now, also, to her great delight, she was dressed as beautifully as any of them, and wore as beautiful jewels. Though she did not know it, she had shrunk to their size, and a very lovely little fairy she made.

Her gown was of white silk, with a long train bordered all round with trails of green ivy, and over her shoulders she wore a long green silk cloak with a little scarlet hood. Her hair looked as though it had been dressed by a Court hairdresser, and amidst the puffs and curls sparkled emeralds and diamonds, like trembling stars. Her little green slippers had silver heels, and diamond buckles on the toes, round her waist hung a diamond girdle, on her neck, too, and fingers gems sparkled and flashed with every movement.

Oh, how proud and delighted Anne did feel, and how eagerly she hoped that she might always live like this! Instead of having one cavalier as most of the ladies had, she had six, but the one with the red feather was her favourite, and hour by hour he and Anne grew more deeply in love with one another.

Unfortunately, though, the other five began to grow very jealous, and they kept such a watch on Anne and her friend, that the poor lovers had no chance to get away and talk by themselves, or exchange even a look, or a kiss, or a handclasp.

However, when people are determined they usually succeed in the end, and one day Anne and her handsome lover managed to slip away unobserved. Hand in hand they ran to a garden which lay at some little distance from the others, one that was seldom used, too, and where the flowers grew so tall and in such profusion that they soon were completely hidden amongst them.

Here they made their home, and here they lived for a time as happily as any two people could who loved each other more than all the world beside.

Alas, though, their happiness was too great to last! They had not been in their beautiful retreat very long, when one day they heard a great noise and disturbance, and to Anne's dismay the five little men followed by a crowd of fairies, equally angered, burst in on them. They had traced the lovers to the garden, and even to the lily-bell in which they had made their home. With drawn swords and faces full of anger, they surrounded the lily and commanded the lovers to come down. Nearly mad with jealousy as they were, they heaped the most cruel and insulting speeches on the poor little pair.

Furious with indignation Anne's lover sprang down, sword in hand, and faced his attackers, but what could one do against such odds? His sword was knocked out of his hand, he himself was overpowered by the numbers who hurled themselves on him. For a while he fought desperately, his back to the wall, his courage unfailing, but the blows fell on him so fast and furious, that in a few minutes he lay bleeding and lifeless at poor Anne's feet.

What happened next Anne never knew. She remembered looking down on her dead lover through eyes almost blind with tears, she remembered seeing his blood staining her dainty green slippers, and splashing her gown, then someone passed a hand over her eyes, and she could see nothing. She was as blind as she had been once before.

All about her she heard strange noises, like the whirring and buzzing of numberless insects; she felt herself being carried through the air at a terrific rate, until her breath was quite taken away,—then she was placed on a seat, and in a moment her sight came back to her.

She was back in the arbour where she had first seen the fairies, but, instead of six little men, she now saw about six-and-twenty big men and women all staring at her with frightened eyes and open mouths.

"She's very bad," they were whispering, "poor maid, she do look ill! 'Tis a fit she's had, and no mistake!" Then seeing her open her eyes and look about her, they crowded nearer. "Why, Anne, child, you've been in a fit, haven't 'ee?"

Anne lifted her arm and looked at it and her hand; there was not a single jewel on either. She glanced down over her gown,—it was of linsey-woolsey, not silk or velvet. She closed her eyes again that they might not see the tears that sprang to them.

"I don't know if I've been in a fit," she said wearily, but to herself she added sadly, "I know, though, that I've been in love."

BARKER AND THE BUCCAS.

Perhaps some of you have never heard about the 'Buccas,' or 'Knockers,' as some people call them, the busy little people about the same size as piskies, who are said to be the souls of the Jews who used to work in the tin mines in Cornwall.

The Buccas live always in rocks, mines, or wells, and they work incessantly pickaxing, digging, sifting, etc., from one year's end to the other, except on Christmas Day, Easter Day, All Saints' Day, and the Jews' Sabbath. On those days their little tools are laid aside, and all is quiet, but on every other you can, if you listen, hear them hammer, hammer, dig, dig, and their tongues chattering all the time.

A lot of these little people lived and worked within the sides of a well in one particular part of Cornwall, the name of which I will not tell you, for in the first place you would not be able to pronounce it if I did; and in the second, you might be tempted to go there and disturb them, which would make them angry, and bring all kinds of ill-luck and trouble upon yourself.

The story I am going to tell you is of someone who did disturb them, and pried upon them after laughing at them. The name of the youth was Barker, a great, idle, hulking fellow, who lived in the neighbourhood of the well where these little Buccas dwelt.

Now this Barker often heard the neighbours talking about the Buccas, and praising their industry, and, like most idle people, he disliked hearing others praised for doing what he knew he ought to do but would not. So, to annoy the neighbours, and the Buccas, too, he declared he "didn't believe there wasn't no such things. Seeing was believing, and when they showed him a Bucca 'twould be soon enough for him to b'lieve there was such things." And he repeated this every time the little men were mentioned.

"'Tis nowt but dreams," he sneered, "there ba'nt no Buccas in Fairy Well, no more nor I'm a Bucca."

"You a Bucca!" cried the neighbours, "why, they wouldn't own such a lazy good-for-nothing. They does more work in a morning than you'd get through in a year, you who never does a hand's-turn for anybody and haven't sense enough to earn your own bread!"

"I've sense enough to find out if there's any such things as Buccas in that there well, and I'll go there and watch and listen till I finds out something, and if there's Buccas there I'll catch one!"

So away he went to spend his time idly lying amidst the tall grass and ferns which grew thickly around the well. This sort of job suited him to a nicety, for the sun was warm and pleasant, and he did no work, for, said he, if he was to work he wouldn't be able to hear any sounds that might come from below. And for once he spoke the truth.

Day after day Barker went and lay by the Fairy Well, and at first he heard never a sound but the birds singing, and the bees humming, and his own breathing. By and by, though, other sounds began to make themselves heard by him, noises of digging and hammering, and numbers of little voices talking and laughing merrily.

Barker could not at first make out what they said, but he could understand that they were always busy. Instead, though, of taking them as an example, the lazy fellow only said to himself gleefully that if others worked so hard, there was the less need for him to do so!

Having discovered that his neighbours were right, and that there really were such people as Buccas, you would have thought that he would have hurried home to tell of his discoveries; but no, he liked the lazy life, lying in the sun by the well, doing nothing. So he kept quiet about his discovery, and every day started off for his favourite spot, making the excuse that he was still watching for Buccas.

As the days passed by he began to understand what the little workmen said, and he gathered from their talk that they worked in sets, and that each set worked for eight hours,—which was, of course, the origin of the Eight Hours Day we hear so much about. He also found that when they had finished they hid away their tools, and every day in a fresh place. I cannot tell you why they hid them, or from whom, unless it was those other 'little people,' the Fairies and Piskies, who love to be up to mischief when they are not doing good. It could not have been from each other that they hid the things, for they talked together about the hiding-places.

One evening, when the day's work was coming to an end, Barker heard the usual discussion begin. "I shall hide mine in this cleft in the rock," said one.

"Very well, then I will hide mine under the ferns."

"Oh," said a third, "I shall leave mine on Barker's knee."

You may be sure it gave Barker quite a shock to hear his own name spoken in those mysterious regions, it frightened him, too, but before he could stir his big, lazy body and run away,—as he meant to do,—he felt three hard blows, bang! whack! bang! and then a heavy weight fell crash upon his knee.

Barker roared and bellowed like a great calf, for the pain was very great, and he was a big coward.

"Take it away! take it away!" he cried, but the only answer was peal upon peal of mocking laughter. "Oh my poor knee, oh my poor knee, I'm lame for life! Take away them tools! Oh my, oh my!" but the more he screamed, the more the Buccas laughed. They laughed and laughed until they were tired, then they vanished, and Master Barker was left to make his way home as best he could. He did not want to tell the neighbours how he got his stiff knee, but pretended he had had a fall; the neighbours, though, soon found out, and pretty well he was laughed at for a long time wherever he went.

Never again did Barker doubt the existence of the Buccas, never again did he speak disrespectfully of them, nor could he forget the lesson he had been taught, for to his dying day he had a stiff knee, and nothing would cure it.

Now, if ever you hear of anyone having 'Barker's knee' you will know that he has spoken rudely of the Buccas, and that the Buccas have paid him out.

LUTEY AND THE MERMAID.

One lovely summer evening many, many years ago, an old man named Lutey was standing on the seashore not far from that beautiful bit of coast called the Lizard.

On the edge of the cliff above him stood a small farm, and here he lived, spending his time between farming, fishing, and, we must admit it, smuggling, too, whenever he got a chance. This summer evening he had finished his day's work early, and while waiting for his supper he strolled along the sands a little way, to see if there was any wreckage to be seen, for it was long since he had had any luck in that way, and he was very much put out about it.

This evening, though, he was no luckier than he had been before, and he was turning away, giving up his search as hopeless, when from somewhere out seaward came a long, low, wailing cry. It was not the melancholy cry of a gull, but of a woman or child in distress.

Lutey stopped, and listened, and looked back, but, as far as he could see, not a living creature was to be seen on the beach but himself. Even though while he listened the sound came wailing over the sand again, and this time left no doubt in his mind. It was a voice. Someone was in trouble, evidently, and calling for help.

Far out on the sands rose a group of rocks which, though covered at high water, were bare now. It was about half ebb, and spring tide, too, so the sea was further out than usual, so far, in fact, that a wide bar of sand stretched between the rocks and the sea. It was from these rocks that the cry seemed to come, and Lutey, feeling sure that someone was out there in distress, turned and walked back quickly to see if he could give any help.

As he drew near he saw that there was no one on the landward side, so he hurried round to the seaward,—and there, to his amazement, his eyes met a sight which left him almost speechless!

Lying on a ledge at the base of the rock, partially covered by the long seaweed which grew in profusion over its rough sides, and partially by her own hair, which was the most glorious you can possibly imagine, was the most beautiful woman his eyes had ever lighted upon. Her skin was a delicate pink and white, even more beautiful than those exquisite little shells one picks up sometimes on the seashore, her clear green eyes sparkled and flashed like the waves with the sun on them, while her hair was the colour of rich gold, like the sun in its glory, and with a ripple in it such as one sees on the sea on a calm day.

This wonderful creature was gazing mournfully out at the distant sea, and uttering from time to time the pitiful cry which had first attracted Lutey's attention. She was evidently in great distress, but how to offer her help and yet not frighten her he knew not, for the roar of the sea had deadened the sound of his footsteps on the soft sand, and she was quite unconscious of his presence.

Lutey coughed and hem'd, but it was of no use—she could not or did not hear; he stamped, he kicked the rock, but all in vain, and at last he had to go close to her and speak.

"What's the matter, missie?" he said. "What be doing all out here by yourself?" He spoke as gently as possible, but, in spite of his gentleness, the lovely creature shrieked with terror, and diving down into the deep pool at the base of the rock, disappeared entirely.

At first Lutey thought she had drowned herself, but when he looked closely into the pool, and contrived to peer through the cloud of hair which floated like fine seaweed all over the top of it, he managed to distinguish a woman's head and shoulders underneath, and looking closer he saw, he was sure, a fish's tail! His knees quaked under him, at that sight, for he realized that the lovely lady was no other than a mermaid!

She, though, seemed as frightened as he was, so he summoned up his courage to speak to her again, for it is always wise to be kind to mermaids, and to avoid offending them, for if they are angry there is no knowing what harm they may do to you.

"Don't be frightened, lady," he said coaxingly; "I wouldn't hurt 'ee for the world, I wouldn't harm a living creature. I only wants to know what your trouble is."

While he was speaking, the maiden had raised her head slightly above the water, and now was gazing at him with eyes the like of which he had never seen before. "I 'opes she understands Carnish," he added to himself, "for 'tis the only langwidge I'm fluent in."

"Beautiful sir," she replied in answer to his thoughts, "we sea-folk can understand all languages, for we visit the coast of every land, and all the tribes of the world sail over our kingdom, and oft-times come down through the waters to our home. The greatest kindness you can do me is to go away. You are accustomed to women who walk, covered with silks and laces. We could not wear such in our world, sporting in the waves, swimming into caverns, clambering into sunken ships. You cannot realize our free and untrammelled existence."

"Now, my lovely lady," said old Lutey, who did not understand a half of what she was saying, "don't 'ee think anything about such trifles, but stop your tears and tell me what I can do for 'ee. For, for sure, I can help 'ee somehow. Tell me how you come'd here, and where you wants to get to."

So the fair creature floated higher in the water, and, gradually growing braver, she presently climbed up and perched herself on the rock where Lutey had first seen her. Her long hair fell about her like a glorious mantle, and she needed no other, for it quite covered her. Holding in her hand her comb and mirror, and glancing from time to time at the latter, she told the old man her story.

"Only a few hours ago," she said sadly, "I was sporting about with my husband and children, as happy as a mermaiden could be. At length, growing weary, we all retired to rest in one of the caverns at Kynance, and there on a soft couch of seaweed my husband laid himself down to sleep. The children went off to play, and I was left alone. For some time I watched the crabs playing in the water, or the tiny fish at the bottom of the pools, but the sweet scent of flowers came to me from the gardens of your world, borne on the light breeze, and I felt I must go and see what these flowers were like whose breath was so beautiful, for we have nothing like it in our dominions. Exquisite sea-plants we have, but they have no sweet perfume.

"Seeing that my husband was asleep, and the children quite happy and safe, I swam off to this shore, but when here I found I could not get near the flowers; I could see them on the tops of the cliffs far, far beyond my reach, so I thought I would rest here for a time, and dress my hair, while breathing in their sweetness.

"I sat on, dreaming of your world and trying to picture to myself what it was like, until I awoke with a start to find the tide far out, beyond the bar. I was so frightened I screamed to my husband to come and help me, but even if he heard me he could not get to me over that sandy ridge; and if he wakes before I am back, and misses me, he will be so angry, for he is very jealous. He will be hungry, too, and if he finds no supper prepared he will eat some of the children!"

"Oh, my dear!" cried Lutey, quite horrified, "he surely wouldn't never do such a dreadful thing!"

"Ah, you do not know Mermen," she said sorrowfully. "They are such gluttons, and will gobble up their children in a moment if their meals are a little late. Scores of my children have been taken from me. That is how it is," she explained, "that you do not oftener see us sea-folk. Poor children, they never learn wisdom! Directly their father begins to whistle or sing, they crowd about him, they are so fond of music, and he gets them to come and kiss his cheek, or whisper in his ear, then he opens wide his mouth, and in they go.—Oh dear, what shall I do! I have only ten little ones left, and they will all be gone if I don't get home before he wakes!"

"Don't 'ee take on so, my dear. The tide will soon be in, and then you can float off as quick as you like."

"Oh, but I cannot wait," she cried, tears running down her cheeks. "Beautiful mortal, help me! Carry me out to sea, give me your aid for ten minutes only, and I will make you rich and glorious for life. Ask of me anything you want, and it shall be yours."

Lutey was so enthralled by the loveliness of the mermaid, that he stood gazing at her, lost in wonder. Her voice, which sounded like a gentle murmuring stream, was to him the most lovely music he had ever heard. He was so fascinated that he would have done anything she asked him. He stooped to pick her up.

"First of all, take this," she said, giving him her pearl comb, "take this, to prove to you that you have not been dreaming, gentle stranger, and that I will do for you what I have said. When you want me, comb the sea three times with this, and call me by my name, 'Morwenna,' and I will come to you. Now take me to the sea."

Stooping again he picked her up in his arms. She clung tightly to him, twining her long, cool arms around his neck, until he felt half suffocated. "Tell me your wishes," she said sweetly, as they went along; "you shall have three. Riches will, of course, be one."

"No, lady," said Lutey thoughtfully, "I don't know that I'm so set on getting gold, but I'll tell 'ee what I should like. I'd dearly love to be able to remove the spells of the witches, to have power over the spirits to make them tell me all I want to know, and I'd like to be able to cure diseases."

"You are the first unselfish man I have met," cried the mermaid admiringly, "you shall have your wishes, and, in addition, I promise you as a reward, that your family shall never come to want."

In a state of great delight, Lutey trudged on with his lovely burthen, while she chatted gaily to him of her home, of the marvels and the riches of the sea, and the world that lay beneath it.

"Come with me, noble youth," she cried, "come with me to our caves and palaces; there are riches, beauty, and everything mortal can want. Our homes are magnificent, the roofs are covered with diamonds and other gems, so that it is ever light and sparkling, the walls are of amber and coral. Your floors are of rough, ugly rocks, ours are of mother-of-pearl. For statuary we have the bodies of earth's most beautiful sons and daughters, who come to us in ships, sent by the King of the Storms. We embalm them, so that they look more lovely even than in life, with their eyes still sparkling, their lips of ruby-red, and the delicate pink of the sea-shell in their cheeks. Come and see for yourself how well we care for them, and how reposeful they look in their pearl and coral homes, with sea-plants growing around them, and gold and silver heaped at their feet. They crossed the world to get it, and their journeys have not been failures. Will you come, noble stranger? Come to be one of us whose lives are all love, and sunshine, and merriment?"

"None of it's in my line, I'm thinking, my dear," said Lutey. "I'd rather come across some of the things that have gone down in the wrecks, wines and brandy, laces and silks; there's a pretty sight of it all gone to the bottom, one time and another, I'm thinking."

"Ah yes! We have vast cellars full of the choicest wines ever made, and caves stored with laces and silks. Come, stranger, come, and take all you want."

"Well," answered the old smuggler, who was thinking what a fine trade he could do, if only he could reach those caves and cellars, "I must say I'd like to, 'tis very tempting, but I should never live to get there, I'm thinking. I should be drownded or smothered before I'd got half-way."

"No, oh no, I can manage that for you. I will make two slits under your chin, your lovely countenance will not suffer, for your beard will hide them. Such a pair of gills is all you want, so do not fear. Do not leave me, generous-hearted youth. Come to the mermaid's home!" They were in the sea by this time, and the breakers they wanted to reach were not far off. Lutey felt strangely tempted to go with this Siren; her flashing green eyes had utterly bewitched him by this time, and her promises had turned his head. She saw that he was almost consenting, almost in her power. She clasped her long, wet, finny fingers more closely round his neck, and pressed her cool lips to his cheeks.

Another instant, and Lutey would have gone to his doom, but at that moment there came from the shore the sound of a dog barking as though in distress. It was the barking of Lutey's own dog, a great favourite with its master. Lutey turned to look. At the edge of the water the poor creature stood; evidently frantic to follow its master, it dashed into the sea and out again, struggling, panting. Beyond, on the cliff, stood his home, the windows flaming against the sun, his garden, and the country round looking green and beautiful; the smoke was rising from his chimney, — ah, his supper! The thought of his nice hot meal broke the spell, and he saw his danger.

"Let me go, let me go!" he shrieked, trying to lower the mermaid to the ground. She only clung the more tightly to him. He felt a sudden fear and loathing of the creature with the scaly body, and fish's tail. Her green eyes no longer fascinated him. He remembered all the tales he had heard of the power of mermaids, and their wickedness, and grew more and more terrified.

"Let me go!" he yelled again, "unwind your gashly great tail from about my legs, and your skinny fingers from off my throat, or I'll—I'll kill you!" and with the same he whipped his big clasp-knife from his pocket.

As the steel flashed before the mermaid's eyes she slipped from him and swam slowly away, but as she went she sang, and the words floated back to Lutey mournfully yet threateningly. "Farewell, farewell for nine long years. Then, my love, I will come again. Mine, mine, for ever mine!"

Poor Lutey, greatly relieved to see her disappear beneath the waves, turned and waded slowly back to land, but so shaken and upset was he by all that had happened, that it was almost more than he could accomplish. On reaching the shore he just managed to scramble to the shed where he kept many of the treasures he had smuggled from time to time, but having reached it he dropped down in a deep, overpowering sleep.

Poor old Ann Betty Lutey was in a dreadful state of mind when supper-time came and went and her husband had not returned. He had never missed it before. All through the night she watched anxiously for him, but when breakfast-time came, and still there was no sign of him, she could not rest at home another minute, and started right away in search of him.

She did not have to search far, though. Outside the door of the shed she found the dog lying sleeping, and as the dog was seldom seen far from his master, she thought she would search the shed first,—and there, of course, she found her husband.

He was still sound asleep. Ann Betty, vexed at once at having been frightened for nothing, shook him none too gently. "Here, Lutey, get up to once, do you hear!" she cried crossly. "Why ever didn't 'ee come in to supper,—such a beautiful bit of roast as I'd got, too! Where've 'ee been? What 'ave 'ee been doing? What 'ave 'ee been sleeping here for?"

Lutey raised himself into a sitting position. "Who are you?" he shouted. "Are you the beautiful maiden come for me? Are you Morwenna?"

"Whatever are you talking about? You haven't called me beautiful for the last thirty years, and I ain't called Morwenna. I'm Ann Betty Lutey, your own lawful wife, and if you don't know me, you must be gone clean out of your mind."

"Ann Betty Lutey," said the old man solemnly, "if you're my lawful wife you've had a narrow escape this night of being left a widow woman, and you may be thankful you've ever set eyes on me again."

"Come in and have some breakfast," said Ann Betty Lutey sternly, "and if you ain't better then I'll send for the doctor. It's my belief your brain is turned."

Lutey got up obediently and went in to his breakfast; indeed, he was glad enough of it, for he was light-headed from want of food. His breakfast did him good. Before he had finished it he was able to tell his wife about his adventure the night before, and he told it so gravely and sensibly that Ann Betty believed every word of it, and no longer thought his brain was turned.

Indeed, she was so much impressed by his story that before many hours had passed she had gone round to every house in the parish spreading the news, and to prove the truth of it she produced the pearl comb.

Then, oh dear, the gossiping that went on! It really was dreadful! The women neglected their homes, their children, and everything else for the whole of that week; and for months after old Lutey was besieged by all the sick and sorry for miles and miles around, who came to him to be cured. He did such a big business in healing people, that not a doctor for miles round could earn a living. Everyone went to old Lutey, and when it was found that he had power over witchcraft, too, he became the most important man in the whole country.

Lutey had been so rude and rough to the mermaiden when he parted from her, that no one would have been surprised if she had avenged herself on him somehow, and punished him severely. But no, she was true to all her promises. He got all his wishes, and neither he nor his descendants have ever come to want. Better far, though, would it have been for him had it been otherwise, for he paid dearly enough for his wishes in the end.

Nine years from that very time, on a calm moonlight night, Lutey, forgetting all about the mermaid and her threats, arranged to go out with a friend to do a little fishing. There was not a breath of wind stirring, and the sea was like glass, so that a sail was useless, and they had to take to the oars. Suddenly, though, without any puff of wind, or anything else to cause it, the sea rose round the boat in one huge wave, covered with a thick crest of foam, and in the midst of the foam was Morwenna!

Morwenna! as lovely as ever, her arms outstretched, her clear green eyes fixed steadily, triumphantly on Lutey. She did not open her lips, or make a sign, she only gazed and gazed at her victim.

For a moment he looked at her as though bewildered, then like one bereft of his senses by some spell, he rose in the boat, and turned his face towards the open sea. "My time is come," he said solemnly and sadly, and without another word to his frightened companion he sprang out of the boat and joined the mermaid. For a yard or two they swam in silence side by side, then disappeared beneath the waves, and the sea was as smooth again as though nothing had happened.

From that moment poor Lutey has never been seen, nor has his body been found. Probably he now forms one of the pieces of statuary so prized by the mermaiden, and stands decked with sea-blossoms, with gold heaped at his feet. Or, maybe, with a pair of gills slit under his chin, he swims about in their beautiful palaces, and revels in the cellars of shipwrecked wines. The misfortunes to his family did not end, though, with Lutey's disappearance, for, no matter how careful they are, how far they live from the sea, or what precautions they take to protect themselves, every ninth year one of old Lutey's descendants is claimed by the sea.

THE WICKED SPECTRE.

There was once upon a time a good old Cornish family of the name of Rosewarne. Well-born, well-to-do gentlepeople they were, who had always lived in their own fine old house on their own estate, and never knew what it was to want any comfort or luxury.

The family in time, though, grew larger than their income, and their pride and their dignity were greater than either, so that in trying to support the large family according to their larger dignity, the poor little income got quite swallowed up and the whole family of Rosewarne became involved in poverty and great difficulties.

Mr. Rosewarne, the father of the last of the family to live on the property, employed for his lawyer and man of business an attorney called Ezekiel Grosse, and, as so often happens, as fast as Mr. Rosewarne went down in the world, his lawyer went up.

Ezekiel grew rich, no one knew how, and prospered in every way; Mr. Rosewarne grew poor, and lost in every way. Nothing on the property paid, and at last, to his great grief and never-ceasing regret, Mr. Rosewarne had to sell his beloved home and everything belonging to him. Then, who should come forward to buy it, as soon as ever it was put up for sale, but his own lawyer, Ezekiel Grosse!

Everybody wondered, and most people declared that Ezekiel could not have made such a large sum honestly by his business; that he must have other and less straight methods of getting money. Anyhow, whether he made it honestly, or dishonestly, he had enough to buy the estate he coveted, and as soon as the old family could turn out, he himself took up his abode in the fine old house, and a very proud man he was.

If, though, he was a proud man as he sat in the spacious library, or wandered through the lofty rooms and noble old hall, he could not have been a very happy one, and very little enjoyment could he have got out of his new possession, for, from the very hour he entered and took up his abode there, such unearthly and mysterious noises, such fearful screams and gruesome groans worried and haunted and dogged him, as made his hair stand on end, and nearly scared him out of his wits. A ghost, too, appeared in the park as soon as night fell.

As Ezekiel crossed the park he would be suddenly confronted by a white, worn face and a pair of great, ghastly, luminous eyes. It would rise up from the ground in front of him, or pop round trees and bushes at him, or, on raising his eyes, he would find it confronting him over a hedge. And before very long the ghost, not content with making noises in the house, and haunting the park, took it into his head to enter the house, and make that his permanent home.

When Ezekiel came face to face with him indoors, he thought he was not such a terrible ghost after all, and much of his fear left him, for the ghost to look at seemed only an infirm old man. Indeed the lawyer found him less terrifying than the horrible uncanny sounds which seemed to come from nowhere, and could not be accounted for.

By and by, though, the ghost's visits were repeated so often, and he began to make such mysterious signs and movements, that the surly lawyer soon lost patience, and before long grew so seriously angry that he determined to put an end to the annoyance and rid himself of his tormentor once and for all.

The very next night as Ezekiel sat alone in his office looking over some papers, and making up his accounts, the ghost glided into the room as usual, and taking up his position opposite, at once began to make the usual mysterious and extraordinary signs. The lawyer was very irritable, he had lost an important case, and was out of spirits, he was unusually nervous, too. For a while he bore the presence of the ghost and his extraordinary behaviour with a certain amount of patience, then suddenly he lost his temper.

"For pity's sake tell me what it is you want with me, and be done with it, can't you?" he cried angrily.

The ghost immediately stopped his gesticulations, and spoke. "Ezekiel Grosse," said he, in a hollow, ghostly voice, "Ezekiel Grosse, follow me. I can show you buried gold, the wealth for which thou longest."

Now no man in the world loved gold better than did the attorney, but he was anything but a brave man, and even he himself knew that he was not a good one, and the thought of going alone with this uncanny guide, to some desolate spot where no one could see or hear him if he called for help, made his teeth chatter and his knees tremble.

He hesitated, and gazed searchingly at the little old ghost, but to save his life he could not utter a word. He nearly suffocated with longing to possess the secret and know where the treasure lay, but he dared not ask; and all the time the spectre stood staring at him with unwinking scornful eyes, as if the sight of the cowardly, trembling man gave him unfeigned pleasure.

At length, beckoning Ezekiel to follow him, he turned and walked towards the door. Then Ezekiel, fearful of losing the secret and the wealth, threw aside every feeling but greed, and sprang to follow—at least, he tried to spring, but so firmly was he secured to his chair he could not budge.

"Come," said the ghost imperatively.

Ezekiel tried again, but great as was his longing to find the gold, he could not obey.

"Gold," whispered the ghost in a whining, craven tone, "don't you hear me, man? Gold!"

"Where?" gasped the lawyer, making another desperate struggle.

"Come with me, and you shall see," answered the spectre, moving further through the doorway; and the lawyer struggled like a madman to get free from the chair and to follow.

"Come, man, come," shrieked the ghost in a perfectly awful voice. "Ezekiel Grosse, I command thee." And with that Ezekiel, by a power stronger than his own, was forced to rise and to follow the old man wheresoever he led him.

Out through the hall they went, down through the park, and on and on by ways the attorney did not know, until at last they arrived at a little dell. The night was pitchy dark, and nothing could Ezekiel see but the ghostly figure gliding along ahead of him, all lit by a weird phosphorescent light. In the dell was a small granite cairn, and here the ghost stopped and looked around for the attorney.

"Ezekiel Grosse," said he, when Ezekiel had come up and was standing on the other side of the cairn. "Ezekiel Grosse, thou longest for gold. So did I! I won the prize, but I found no pleasure in it. Beneath those stones lies treasure enough to make thee richer than thou hast ever dreamed of. Dig for it, it is yours. Obtain it and keep it all to yourself, and be one of the rich men of the earth, and when thou art happiest I will come and look upon you."

With that the spectre disappeared, and Ezekiel, overcome with fright and amazement, was left alone by the cairn.

"Well," he said at last, recovering his courage, "I don't care if you are ghost or devil, I will soon find out if you are telling me lies or not!" A harsh laugh sounded through the darkness, as though in answer to his brave words, and once again the attorney trembled with fear.

He did not begin his search that night, but taking careful note of the exact spot, he returned to his house to think over all that had happened; and what he decided was that he was not going to let any squeamishness stand in the way of a fortune.

"I'll tip over that old cairn," he said, with a great show of coolness, "and I'll search every foot of ground under it and around it, and it shall not be my fault if the treasure is not found!"

So, a night or two later, armed with a crowbar and other tools, away he started secretly, and found his way again to the lonely dell, where he soon dispersed the stones of the cairn and began his digging. The ground was hard and flinty, and the work anything but easy, but he had not far to dig before he came across something, something hard and round, which increased his excitement until it nearly suffocated him.

Feverishly he dug and dug, and cleared away the earth until at last he had laid bare a large metallic urn sunk deep in the ground, an urn so large and heavy that though he used his utmost strength, and his strength by that time was almost that of a madman, he could not move it, much less carry it home with him; and having brought no light he could not even examine it. So all he could do that night was to cover it over again with earth, and replace the stones on the top so that no one, coming upon it, should guess that the cairn had been touched. Ezekiel scarcely knew how to live through the next twenty-four hours, and as soon as it was dark on the following evening he crept out of his house, with a dark lantern concealed beneath his cloak.

He knew his way to the dell so well now that he reached there very quickly, and with very little trouble he threw down the cairn and laid bare the urn again. By the light of the lantern he soon forced open the lid, in spite of the trembling of his eager, covetous fingers. The lid off he went to plunge his hand in boldly, when to his unspeakable delight he found the thing full to the brim of gold coins of all sorts and sizes, and from all countries, coins of the rarest and most valuable description!

Glancing round every now and then to see that he was not followed, or that no one had come upon him accidentally, he loaded every pocket in his clothing with his treasure, then he buried the urn, rebuilt the cairn, and hurried back to his house anxious to conceal his wealth in a place of safety.

From that time forward, whenever he could get out without arousing the suspicions of his servants, he went night after night to the cairn, until he had brought away every coin, and had them all carefully hidden in Rosewarne House.

And now, his treasure safe, himself the richest man in the county, Ezekiel Grosse began to feel perfectly happy. He built new wings on to the old house, he laid out the gardens, and made improvements everywhere; even in his own clothing and his personal appearance.

The people round could not help noticing the changes that were taking place, the money that was being spent, and the improvements that were being made. You may be quite sure, too, that the attorney took care to parade his wealth, for, having money, a fine house, fine clothes, and carriages and servants, indeed, everything but friends, he began to want friends too, and people to whom to show off his grandeur.

And before very long, though everyone knew his character, and what he had been and what he had done, the neighbouring gentry began to seek his acquaintance, and many of them declared themselves his friends.

After that the attorney broke forth in quite a new way, he began to give entertainments more lavish and splendid than anything of the kind ever known in the county. Everyone flocked to him, people plotted and struggled to get invitations from him. They quite ignored the fact that but a little while before he had been a poor rogue of an attorney whom they all despised, and that he had come by his wealth by means which no one had been able to fathom. They all seemed to be bewitched, to be under some spell.

High revels were constantly held at Rosewarne House, now, and the gayest and liveliest of all the people gathered there was the master himself. He was as happy at this time as a man could be, and a great part of his happiness was due to the fact that he had never set eyes on his ghostly visitor since the night he conducted him to the treasure in the dell.

Months went by, the feastings and gaieties grew more and more splendid, the hospitality more and more profuse, those who had not his acquaintance, craved it, and everyone bowed before the 'Lord of Rosewarne,' as in time he came to be called.

Indeed, he went about as though he were the lord of the whole county, and everyone his inferior. He travelled always in a chaise and four, he kept numberless carriages, horses, servants. He was elected to every high position in the county, and he was never tired of preaching of the beauty of honesty and uprightness, and our duty to our poorer brethren.

So things went on until one Christmas Eve, when there was gathered at Rosewarne a large company of the most beautiful and well-born of all the families in Cornwall. Such a gathering had seldom been seen as was gathered that night in the great hall for the ball Ezekiel Grosse was giving; and in the kitchen was an equally large party engaged in the same form of enjoyment.

Food and wine were provided in lavish profusion, everything was on a most sumptuous scale. Merriment ran high, everyone was in the gayest of spirits, and gayest of all was Ezekiel. Now he felt the power of wealth, now he was positive that all other things were as nothing to it; for had it not made him the most popular, the most important, the most welcomed and sought-after man in the county?

All had just reached the very highest pitch of mirth and excitement that could be reached, when a sudden chill, as though the hand of death were on them, fell on the company! The dancing ceased, no one quite knew why, and the dancers looked at each other uneasily, each frightened by the other's pallor.

Then, suddenly, whence, or how come, no one knew,—in the middle of the hall they saw a little old man standing gazing at the host with eyes from which darted a hatred which was perfectly venomous. Everyone wanted to ask who he was, and how he had come, but no one dared. They looked at Ezekiel Grosse, expecting him in his usually haughty way to demand what right he had there;—but Ezekiel Grosse stood like a figure hewn out of stone.

It all took place in about a minute, and then the old man vanished in the same mysterious way that he had come.

As soon as he had gone, the host, who a moment before had been petrified with terror, as quickly recovered himself, and burst into uproarious laughter. It was forced laughter, though, unnatural mirth, as most of those present could not help feeling.

"Ha, ha! my friends. What do you think of my little surprise? How do you like my Father Christmas? Cleverly managed, was it not? But you all look rather alarmed by his sudden movements. I hope my little joke has not frightened you. Hand round the wine and punch there, then we will on with the dancing again!"

Try as he would, though, he could not put new life into the evening's festivities, the mirth was dead, the pleasure overcast, for there was still that strange deathlike chill in the air. The guests, frightened, and convinced that something was wrong, made various excuses and one by one took their departure.

From that evening everything was changed. Ezekiel Grosse and his entertainments were never the same again. He never acknowledged any difference, and he gave more parties, and issued more invitations than ever, but at every feast, every dance, every entertainment of any sort, there was always one uninvited guest, a little wizened, weird old man, who sat back in his chair and never spoke to anyone, but gazed all the time at Ezekiel with stern, uncanny eyes which frightened all who caught sight of them. Indeed, the effect he had on the guests was extraordinary; under the chill of his presence they could not talk, or eat or drink, or keep up any appearance of enjoyment.

Ezekiel was the bravest of them. He tried to encourage them to talk and laugh,—talking and laughing loudly himself all the time, but all was unnatural. His apologies for his strange visitor were numerous. He was an old friend who liked to come to him and see new faces and young life, but was too old to do more than look on. He was deaf and dumb, that was why his conduct was so strange. Sometimes the little old man sat unmoved while these stories were told, at other times, though, he would spring up, and with a burst of mocking laughter would disappear no one knew how.

By and by, of course, Ezekiel Grosse's friends began to leave him. They declined his invitations, and omitted to include him in theirs, so that in a comparatively short time he had not a single friend remaining of all those he had spent so much upon.

Disappointed and miserable, he soon became the wreck of his old self. Alone in his luxurious house now, save for his old clerk John Cull, he could never be said to be quite alone, either, for wherever he went, or whatever he did, the spectre haunted him persistently. Under this persecution the attorney became a brokendown, miserable man, with every feature stamped with terror. For a long time he bore with the merciless ghost without complaining, but at last he came to an end of his endurance. In heart-rending terms, with tears and piteous pleading, he begged the old man to go away and leave him. He had been punished sufficiently, he said. But his prayers were poured into deaf ears. The spectre absolutely refused to go, and for some time stuck to his word. Then, at last he consented, on one condition, and that was that Ezekiel should give up all his wealth to someone the spectre should name.

"Who am I to give it to?" gasped Ezekiel humbly.

"To John Cull, the man you have overworked and underpaid for years. John Cull, your clerk and dependent."

Ezekiel Grosse had been given wealth, happiness, friends, only to be deprived of all, to be lowered in the eyes of all men, with not one to pity him. This was the punishment designed by the frightful spectre, who was no more nor less than an ancestor of the family Ezekiel Grosse had robbed, the Rosewarnes. He had planned to punish the lawyer by whose wickedness his family had been robbed and made homeless, and he carried through his plan.

Poor Ezekiel Grosse did not live long in his disappointment and shame. He was found dead one day, with strange marks upon him, and people who saw it say that when he died the weird little spectre stood beside him with a pleased smile on his face. As soon as it was dark, he disappeared, and the story goes that he took Ezekiel's body with him, for from that day to this it has never been seen.

THE STORY OF THE LOVERS' COVE.

This is a sad story,—at least, some will think it sad! It is not about fairies, or giants, or witches, but about two lovers who loved each other above and beyond everything else in the world;— which is uncommon, for most people love themselves in that way first, and someone else next.

These two lovers loved each other passionately and devotedly. They used to meet in the Lovers' Cove, or Porthangwartha,—which means the same,— and many a happy meeting they had, and well did everything go until they told their friends. After that there was such a talk and such a stir, and such hardness and misery, that the lovers never again knew what it was to be happy. The parents said that they should not love each other,—which was foolish, for they could not prevent it; that they should never meet and never marry, which was cruel, for this they could prevent, and did. So the poor lovers led a life of utter wretchedness, for they were persecuted sadly, and were breaking their hearts for each other.

At last their persecutors ended by driving the young man away. He determined to go to the West Indies. Then the relations congratulated themselves heartily that they had got their own way, and parted the lovers for ever.

In spite of all their precautions, though, those two poor heart-broken lovers managed to meet once more; and as it was to be their very last sight of each other for they did not know how long, perhaps for ever, it was a very, very sad parting indeed.

It was in the Lovers' Cove that they met, and there, under the frosty light of the moon, they bade each other their sad good-byes, and while they clung to each other for the last time, they made a solemn vow that, living or dead, they would meet again in that same place at that same hour of the same day three years hence.

So the young man sailed away, and the girl lived with her parents, going about her duties quietly and patiently, and, in spite of her sadness, with a look of hope in her eyes that increased and increased as the weeks and months slipped by. Her parents noticed it, and told themselves that she had forgotten the banished lover, and would soon learn to care for one of those they approved of. When, though, she had refused to listen to any of the others who came wooing her, they began to fear that they were mistaken, and were puzzled to know what it was that was driving the wistfulness from her face, and the languor from her step.

So the long years dragged to a close, and at last, as it was bound to do, the end of the three years drew very near, and with each day the girl's step grew lighter and more buoyant, her eyes glistened and her lips curved in a smile that was new to them. Now and then even a snatch of song burst from them. Her parents had no doubt now that she had quite forgotten the lover whose name had not been mentioned in her presence since the day he sailed.

Then, at last, the three years were really past and gone, the last day dawned and wore away to evening, and then night fell, moonlit, still, beautiful, a fitting night for lovers who were to meet once more, whether living or dead. In the Cove it was as light as day, one could count each wave as it rose and fell, and see distinctly the white foam at its edge as it broke on the beach. The sands gleamed like silver in the sad white light save where the rocks threw dark shadows.

All round the coast the witches and wizards were busy manufacturing their spells. High up on a cliff overlooking the Lovers' Cove an old woman,— not a witch,—was sitting preparing her herbs and simples,—which must always be done by moonlight,—when suddenly she was startled to see down in the Cove below her the figure of the maiden swiftly crossing the sands. The old dame, who recognized the girl, was startled for it was nearly twelve o'clock, and in that part most people are in bed by nine.

Swiftly and unhesitatingly the girl made her way to a rock far out on the sands, and close to the water. Up the rock she climbed, and sat herself down as though it had been noon on a fine summer's day. Did not she know, wondered the old woman nervously, that the tide was rapidly rising, and the rock being fast surrounded? Apparently, though, the maiden did not know, or care, for there she sat immovable, her face turned towards the sea, gazing at it with bright intent eyes, as though searching its face for something.

At last the old woman grew so alarmed she could endure the suspense no longer. The girl's danger increased every moment, and she felt it her duty to go and warn her, and give her what help she could. So with trembling limbs and fast-beating heart she hurried as fast as she was able down the side of the cliff. The path, though, was rough and winding, and she was old. At one point the end of the beach where the girl sat was cut off from her view. It was only for a moment, certainly, yet when the old dame caught sight of her again, she saw, to her amazement, that a fine young sailor had also mounted the rock, and was seated close beside her!

He too, sailor though he was, seemed quite unconscious of their danger. They sat there on the water-surrounded rock, he with arm around the girl, she with her head on his breast, oblivious of everything but each other.

"Oh ho! my young woman!" said the old dame to herself, "so this is how you pass your time while your lover is away! and after the way you pretended to love him, too!" She felt quite cross, for she was very tired and very frightened and in no mood to smile at lovers' foolishness. She sat herself down on a rock by the path they would have to ascend, determined to await their return, partly to give the maiden a good sound scolding for her reckless behaviour, and partly to satisfy her curiosity by seeing who the young man was who had won her heart away from the absent lover.

The lovers, though, appeared in no hurry to move. There they sat clinging together, with the moon shining down coldly on them, and the water gleaming around them. The wind had died away until there seemed to be scarcely a breath of air stirring, and the sea lay as calm as a lake. The whole scene resembled Fairyland, with the lovers as two spirits watching over the Cove. The tide rose higher and higher, and the only sound to be heard in that lone, desolate spot was the lazy plash of the waves on the shore, and around the cliffs.

In a short time the water rose so high that the rock was almost covered; to get off it now the lovers would have to swim; yet still they paid no heed. They seemed lost to everything but each other.

It was all so ghostly and uncanny that the poor old woman grew wild with nervousness and excitement. She called and called to them at the top of her voice, but she failed to make it reach them. The plash of the waves and the sighing of the gently heaving sea seemed to swallow it up. And when at last a wave came up and washed right over them, she shrieked aloud, distracted by her own helplessness, and covered her eyes with her apron. She could not bear to look and watch them being drowned.

With her face hidden she waited, breathless, for their shrieks for help,— but none came. She uncovered her eyes and looked at the rock,—it was bare, save for the water which now covered it. She gazed frantically around, first at the beach, then out to sea; the beach was empty, save for herself, but out on the sea were the two lovers, floating out on the scarcely moving waters, hand in hand, gazing into each other's eyes, smiling happily and without sign of struggle. Further and further away they drifted. Then across the still waters came the sound of sweet low voices singing, and in the stillness which hung over everything the very words sounded distinctly:—

Slowly, slowly they passed out through the moonlit sea, sweetly chanting their pathetic song; until at last they turned and faced the shore; and in that moment the old woman recognized in the sailor the lonely maiden's lover, who had been driven away by her parents so long before.

One long look they took at the Lovers' Cove and the black rock on which they had met, then turned their happy faces to each other, their lips meeting in one long, long kiss, and while their lips were meeting they sank quickly beneath the waves.

A few days later the maiden's body was found not far from the Lovers' Cove; and some time after news reached the village that on the very night that she had been seen with him on the rock he had been killed in a foreign land.

THE SILVER TABLE.

Off Cudden Point, in the parish of Perranuthnoe, there lies buried in the sea, treasure enough to make anyone who finds it, one of the wealthiest persons in the whole county.

Now and then, during the spring-tides, when the water is very low, small portions of it are found, just enough to keep up the excitement, and cause dozens of children from all the neighbourhood round to gather there in a swarm, to search among the seaweeds, and dig in the sands, and venture out in the sea itself as far as they dare. It is only about once in a blue moon that they do come upon treasure, but there is always the hope that any hour or day may bring them a big find.

Jewellery and coins, and silver goblets, are some of the treasures they seek, but the greatest of all is no less a thing than a table, a large and massive table, too, made of solid silver.

I am sure you would like to know why they expect such a prize, so I will tell you.

Many, many years ago there lived in those parts a very wealthy man. He was also a very wicked one, indeed it was said that he was no other than the Lord of Pengerswick, of whom you will have read in another of these stories. It was rather difficult to say for certain, for the wicked old man being an enchanter could go about in all kinds of disguises, so that only those who had the gift of 'second sight' could discover him.

Anyhow, if this rich, bad man was not the Lord of Pengerswick he was someone just as wicked, and just as rich. I believe, though, it was that old enchanter, and, at any rate, we will call him so for the time.

The old gentleman had plenty of money and he spent it freely too, for it cost him no trouble to get. He ground it out of the poor, and in the most cruel manner. As he got it so easily he did not mind wasting it, and he kept 'open house' as they call it,—that is, he always had a houseful of visitors, men and women who were nearly as bad as he was, and he provided them with every kind of luxury, and pleasure, and amusement that he could think of. They rode pell-mell over the country on fiery, unmanageable horses, breaking down the farmers' hedges, trampling down the land, hunting, shooting, dancing and gambling! They did anything and everything that was wild, and foolish, and exciting, in order to make the days pass pleasantly.

One very, very hot summer's day, though, when the sun was pouring down pitilessly, scorching up everything, and there was scarcely a breath of air to be found, and it was too hot to dance, or to ride, or do anything tiring, this gay crew thought they would like to spend some hours on the sea, where it was cooler than on the land.

So the Lord of Pengerswick, always glad to show off his possessions, ordered his largest and most sumptuous barge to be set afloat, and stored with every kind of luxury, and every sort of dainty thing he could think of, and the gay party went on board. Seated on silken cushions under an awning of cloth of gold, they began at once to feast on the marvellous dainties spread for them on a large solid silver table, and all the time they feasted and laughed and jested, delicate music and singing wafted towards them from the far end of the boat, to charm their ears if they cared to listen.

While, though, the awning sheltered them from the sun, it also concealed from them a little cloud which presently appeared in the sky; and the music, talk and laughter drowned the sound of a little breeze that sighed round the vessel.

The little breeze sighed, and went away unnoticed, but presently returned, not little now, but very big, and determined to be heard; but they were, by this time, making such a noise on board, that even the louder breeze went unheeded, until, grown quite angry, in a gust of fury it struck the boat—and what happened next no one knows, for none were left to tell the tale,—except the breeze, and he went scuffling off to another point.

This only is known, that where the barge had floated nothing was to be seen but a desolate expanse of water, but for years and years afterwards, when the wind was in the right direction, the fishermen heard sounds of laughter and talking coming up from the bottom of the sea, the rattle of plates and the jingle of glasses, and through it all the strains of sweet music, and deep voices singing. If the moon was in the right quarter and the water very still, far down beneath the waves could be seen the gleaming silver table, and the wicked old Lord of Pengerswick and his guests still seated round it keeping up their revels.

The feasting must all have ceased by this time, though, for no sound is ever heard now, and it is long since anyone has caught sight of the pleasure-loving crew. A part of the treasure has been cast up by the sea, and seized by the descendants of the poor people the old lord robbed, and it seems quite possible that if they only wait long enough, and the tide goes out far enough, someone will be so fortunate as to find the silver table.

CRUEL COPPINGER, THE DANE.

One of the most terrific storms ever known was raging on the north coast of Cornwall. The gale, blowing up channel from the southwest, broke with such fury on that bold, unsheltered piece of coast by Morwenstow, that the wreckers, who were gathered on the shore and heights above, had more than enough to do to keep their feet. The rain came down in driving sheets, shutting off the sea from their eager eyes, so that they could see nothing of the prey they were watching for.

Beaten down, drenched, well-nigh frozen, even these hardy men were on the point of giving way before the fury of the hurricane, when suddenly from out the sheets of driving rain loomed a vessel, a foreigner. If she had been a phantom ship, as at first they thought she must be, she could not have appeared more strangely, suddenly, or unexpectedly. But it was no phantom battling so bravely, yet so hopelessly with the fierce waves, ploughing her way through them, defying their efforts to draw her down and devour her. She rolled and lurched heavily, and was driven closer and closer on to the jagged rocks of that cruel coast; her sails were in rags, and she herself was utterly beyond control.

As she drew nearer, the terror-stricken faces of those on board could be plainly seen, clinging to each other or to the masts, praying, gesticulating, or too frightened to do anything but gaze with fixed and ghastly eyes at the awful fate awaiting them.

Standing near the wheel was a man who, even at such a time, seemed to hold himself apart from the rest. He was of gigantic size, towering above the heads of the rest of them. He had stripped himself of his clothing, and was evidently awaiting a suitable moment to plunge off the vessel into the boiling ocean, and fight his hand-to-hand battle with death. At last the right moment came. Without an instant's hesitation he plunged over the side into the raging waters. Then rising again, in a moment or two, to the surface, like a perfect Hercules, he fought his way through the billows, his strong arm and massive chest defying their power. On, on he went, now riding on the top of a huge boiling mountain of water, now down in the hollow, with the raging sea rising above him, so that it seemed he must be swallowed and crushed in their embrace.

Long the struggle continued, and the excitement on shore grew intense, for no one thought it possible that he could reach the land alive. But, after a terrible fight which would have exhausted anyone not endowed with supernatural powers, his bravery was rewarded, and with one tremendous leap he landed safely on the shore, well beyond the deadly clutch of the waves.

All the people of the country-side seemed now to have gathered to witness the marvellous combat, men and women, on horse and on foot, wreckers, fishermen, and what not,—and into the midst of them all rushed the dripping stranger. Apparently not in the least exhausted, he snatched the scarlet cloak off the shoulders of an old woman, and wrapping it about himself, as suddenly sprang up behind a young woman, who was sitting on her horse watching the wreck, and urging the animal on to a furious gallop, rode off in the direction of the young woman's home. The people shouted and screamed, for they thought the poor girl was being carried off, no one knew where, by the Evil One himself; but the strange cries, which they took to be the language of the Lower Regions, were only a foreign tongue, and the horse made for its own stable by instinct.

When Miss Dinah Hamlyn and her reeking steed dashed into the courtyard of her own home, closely clasped by a tall wicked-looking man wrapped in a scarlet cloak, the outcry was doubled. There was nothing to be done, though, but to give the stranger a suit of Mr. Hamlyn's clothes, and some food, and very comely he looked in the long coat, the handsome waistcoat, knee-breeches, and buckled shoes.

He accepted the clothes, and the food, and indeed all their attention, as a matter of course, and having informed them that his name was Coppinger, and that he was a Dane, he seemed to think he had done all that was required of him, and settled down in the family circle as though he were one of them, and as welcome as though he were an old family friend.

Of the distressed vessel, and the rest of the shipwrecked crew, nothing more was seen from the moment the big man left her. How or where she disappeared no one knew, all eyes had been fixed on the struggling swimmer from the moment he leapt into the sea; and when they had looked again the ship had gone, and no trace or sign of her or her crew was ever found on that coast, or on any other.

At first Coppinger made himself most agreeable to the people he had appeared amongst, he was pleasant and kind beyond anything you can imagine. Miss Dinah Hamlyn thought him a very attractive man, indeed, and not only forgave him for his first treatment of her, but thought it something to be proud of. Old Mr. Hamlyn liked the man, too, and was as kind to him as could be, giving him the best he had, and even at last consenting to his marriage with Miss Dinah herself, though against his own feelings.

Coppinger had given out that he was a Dane of noble birth and great wealth, who had run away to escape marrying a lady he disliked. Old Farmer Hamlyn did not like his daughter to marry a 'furriner,' and he considered that people should marry in their own stations; but Dinah herself loved the man all the better for what he had told them, and between them they soon overcame the father's scruples, and the wedding-day was fixed.

The wedding-day had to be postponed, though, for Farmer Hamlyn fell ill, grew rapidly worse, and in a very short time was dead and buried. As soon as this was over a great change came over things. Master Coppinger began to show himself in his true character, and a very black character indeed his was! So black and so bad that for generations his mere name was a terror to the people who lived in that part of the world, and is detested to this day.

As soon as poor Farmer Hamlyn had passed away, Coppinger made himself master and controller of the house and all in it, even to the smallest domestic affairs. Dinah he persuaded to marry him at once, and hardly had she done so, when all the evil in his character made itself known, and as though to make up for having so long suppressed his wicked passions, he utterly threw off all appearance of goodness or respectability, and poor respectable Farmer Hamlyn's quiet, happy home became a den of thieves and vagabonds, and a meeting-place for all the lawless characters in the county.

Then it very soon came out that the whole country-side was infested with a body of smugglers, wreckers, poachers, robbers, and murderers, over all of whom 'Cruel Coppinger,' as he came to be called by the honest people in the neighbourhood, was captain and ringleader.

He and his gang worked their own wicked will, and the poor inhabitants of the place were completely in their power, for there were no magistrates, or rich men of power in that part, and no revenue officer dared show himself. The clergyman was scared into silence, and Coppinger and his band ruled the country-side.

Very soon a regular system of smuggling was carried on. All sorts of strange vessels appeared on that part of the coast, and were guided by signals to a safe creek or cove, where they were unloaded, and the valuable, illegal spoil brought in and hidden in the huge caves, which no one but Coppinger and his crew dared to enter, for it would have meant torture and death.

By and by one particular vessel, the 'Black Prince,' Coppinger's own, which he had had built for him in Denmark, became a perfect terror to all the other vessels in the parts she frequented. Coppinger and his crew sailed the seas as though they belonged to them, robbing, murdering, and doing every evil thing they could think of.

If a vessel chased them, they led her into such dangerous parts of the coast that her whole crew invariably perished, while the 'Black Prince' glided out by some intricate passage, and got safely off. If one of the poor landsmen offended any of the gang, away he was dragged to Coppinger's vessel, and there made to serve until he was ransomed, and as the people were almost reduced to beggary by the rogues, there was very little chance of the poor fellow's ever being free again.

Wealth poured into their clutches, and Coppinger soon began to have enormous quantities of gold, which he spent lavishly. Amongst other things he bought a farm, which bordered on the sea, but the lawyer to whom he was to pay the money was taken aback at receiving it in coins from pretty nearly every country in the world, doubloons, ducats, dollars, pistoles! At first he refused to accept them, but a look from Coppinger, and a threat, made him change his mind. He accepted the coins without another word, and handed over the papers.

Of course, when Coppinger realized his power, and saw how everyone feared him, he grew more and more daring. He closed up bridle-paths, to which he had no possible right, and made new ones, where he had no right to make them, and forbade anyone but his own friends to use them after a certain hour in the evening, and no one dared disobey him. Their roads were called 'Coppinger's Tracks,' and all met at a headland called 'Steeple Brink,' a huge hollow cliff which ran three hundred feet sheer up from the beach, while the vast, roomy cave beneath it ran right back into the land. Folks said it was as large as Kilkhampton Church, and they were not far wrong.

This was called 'Coppinger's Cave,' and here took place such scenes of wickedness and cruelty as no one can imagine in these days. Here all the stores were kept, wines, spirits, animals, silks, gold, tea, and everything of value that they could lay hands on. No one but the crew ever dared to show themselves there, for it was more than their lives were worth, the crew being bound by a terrible oath to help their captain in any wickedness he might choose to perpetrate. So it came to pass that all, whether of his band or not, gave in to him, and were ruled by him as though they were slaves and he their lord.

His own house, too, was full of misery and noisy, disgraceful scenes. When John Hamlyn died, Coppinger had obtained possession somehow of everything belonging to him, with the exception of a large sum of money which went to the widow. Coppinger meant to have this money too, though, so he began by getting small sums from his mother-in-law from time to time, until she at last refused to give him any more, and even his threats and coaxings failed to move her.

Cruel Coppinger was not a man to be baulked in any way, so he soon hit upon a plan. Taking his wife to her room, he tied her to the post of the great bedstead, then calling in her mother he told her that he was going to flog Dinah with the cat-o'-nine-tails which he held in his hand, until she handed over to him the money he had asked her for. They knew quite well that he would be as good as his word, and that refusal meant death by torture to Dinah; so the poor mother was compelled to give in, and finding that this plan answered his purpose so well, he repeated the performance until he had had nearly every penny poor old Mrs. Hamlyn was possessed of.

Amongst the numerous animals he owned, there was one favourite mare, —a vicious, uncontrollable creature,—on which he used to scour the country at a terrible pace, spreading terror wherever he went. He never cared in the least how many people or animals he knocked over and trampled to death; the more weak and helpless they were the more he seemed to love to hurt them.

One evening, after spending a few festive hours at a neighbour's house, he was just on the point of departing when he happened to notice seated by the hearth a poor little half-witted tailor, who always went by the name of 'Uncle Tom.'

Uncle Tom was a very quiet, extremely nervous little man, well-known and pitied by all. He went from house to house all over the countryside, doing a day's work at one house, and half a day's at another, and in most houses he was given a meal in addition to his trifling pay, for everyone liked him, he was always willing and obliging, and had never harmed anyone in his life.

"Hulloa, Uncle Tom!" cried Coppinger boisterously, going up and laying a heavy hand on the thin, shaking shoulder of the little tailor. "We are both bound for the same direction. Come along with me, I'll give you a lift on my mare."

The old man shrank away nervously, mumbling all sorts of excuses, for he above all people lived in deadly terror of Cruel Coppinger, also of his vicious mare, and the idea of being at the mercy of them both nearly scared away what few wits he had.

The sight of his terror, though, only made Coppinger more determined to frighten him. He loved to torment so helpless a victim, and the other people present, partly from love of mischief, but chiefly to please Coppinger, egged the tormentor on.

In spite of his struggles and entreaties they hoisted the poor little tailor on to the back of the prancing, restive beast, and held him there while Coppinger sprang up.

No sooner were they both mounted than up reared the mare, danced round on her hind legs a time or two, and then sprang away along the road at a rate which it made one gasp to witness. Tom clung in sheer terror to his big tormentor, afraid of falling off, yet afraid to stay on. Coppinger, guessing perhaps that the little man in his terror might spring off, undid his belt, and passed it round the little tailor's body, buckling it securely around them both. Then, having fastened his victim to him, beyond all hope of escape, he urged the mare on to a more furious pace than ever. They tore through the air at lightning speed. Tom shrieked and prayed to be put down,—to be told whither he was to be taken,—what Coppinger meant to do with him; and pleaded to be killed at once, rather than tortured. They dashed on past his own little cottage, and his wife at the door, catching sight of the pair, nearly fainted to see her poor husband in the grasp of the tyrant. On they went and on, without sign of stopping. They leapt ditches and hedges, animals, waggons, people, anything that came in their way, until, coming at last to a steep hill, they slackened their pace a little, and Coppinger condescended to speak.

"I promised the Devil I would bring him a tailor," he said, "for his clothes sadly need mending, and I am going to carry you to him to-night. It will not be very hard work, and he won't harm you as long as you do what he bids you."

So terrified was poor little Uncle Tom on hearing this awful fate, that he had a fit then and there from fright, and the violence of his struggles was such that the belt gave way, and he was flung from the racing mare, right into the ditch by the roadside.

There he lay all night, and there he was found in the morning, not only battered and bruised and half frozen, but with his poor weak mind quite gone.

"He would never sew for the Devil," he kept repeating over and over and over again, "he would never sew for the Devil, nor for Coppinger either. He believed Coppinger was the Devil, and he might do his work himself, Uncle Tom would never work for such as he!"

Never again did poor Uncle Tom get back his reason, or do another stroke of work to support himself and his wife,—but Coppinger had had his joke, and thought it a very fine one.

Countless were the cruel pranks he played on the poor, the helpless, and defenceless, until at last people became afraid to go outside their houses, and were afraid to stay in them, for every day brought some new wickedness done by him, and every fresh one was worse than the last.

Coppinger had one child, a boy; he was deaf and dumb, and as uncanny a child as his father was a man. He was a beautiful boy to look at, with soft fair skin and golden hair, but he had his father's cruel eyes, and his father's cruel nature. From his babyhood his mischievousness and wickedness knew no bounds; any bird, or animal, or even child that came within his reach he would torment almost to death, and the more his victim writhed and screamed, the greater was his delight.

When he was but six he was found one day on the headland, dancing in frantic joy, and pointing with gestures of delight to the beach below. Hurrying down they found the mangled and bleeding corpse of a little child, his companion, whom he had enticed to the edge of the cliff, and, by an unexpected push, sent headlong on to the rocks beneath. From that day he was always to be found on the tragic spot, and when a stranger passed he would make unearthly sounds of delight, and pointing down to the beach, dance and throw himself about in ecstasy.

All this time Coppinger and his gang grew more and more reckless and daring, until they were the scourge of the country-side. To what lengths they might have gone, no earthly powers can tell, but money became scarce, and times grew bad for them. Armed King's cutters came, not singly, but in great numbers, and tidings of danger were brought to Cruel Coppinger by strangely dressed foreigners.

And so, at last, things came to a climax, and deliverance was at hand for the poor suffering people.

Just such another time as preceded Coppinger's arrival, burst again on that coast; the rain and hail came down in sheets, the gale blew furiously all day. At sunset a vessel appeared off the coast—full-rigged.

Presently a rocket went up from the Gull Rock,—a little rock island with a creek on the landside, a spot where many smugglings had taken place. A gun answered from the ship, again both signals were sent up. Then, on the topmost peak of the rock, appeared the huge form of Coppinger. He waved his sword, and a boat immediately put off from the ship, with two men at each oar, for the tide is terribly strong just there. They neared the rock, rode boldly through the surf, and were steered into the Gull Creek by someone who evidently knew the coast well.

Then Coppinger, who was standing impatiently awaiting them, leapt on board and took the command.

Their efforts to get back to the vessel were enormous. Like giants they laboured at their oars to force a path through the boiling, seething waters. Once, as they drew off-shore, one of the rowers, either from loss of strength or of courage, relaxed his hold for a moment; in an instant a cutlass waved above his head, and one swift cruel stroke cut him down. It was the last brutal deed that Cruel Coppinger was ever seen to do.

He and his men reached the ship and got on board. What happened afterwards no one knows, for at the same moment she disappeared like some ghostly, phantom ship, nobody knows where or how.

Then, in even more fearful violence than before, the storm raged and beat on that coast. Hail, thunder, lightning, hurricanes of wind blinded, deafened, or killed all who were exposed to it.

Round Coppinger's home it expended the very utmost of its fury; trees were torn up by the roots, the thatch was blown off the outhouses, chimneys fell, windows were blown in, and, as Dinah, terrified by the uproar and destruction racing round her, stood holding her uncanny child in her arms, through the roof and ceiling came crashing a monstrous thunderbolt, surrounded by flames, and fell hissing at the very foot of Cruel Coppinger's chair.

MADGE FIGGY, THE WRECKER.

Those of you who know Land's End, and that part of it called Tol-pedn-penwith, cannot fail to have been struck by a huge cliff there, in shape like a ladder, or flight of steps, formed of massive blocks of granite, piled one upon another, and on the top of which there is perched what looks like, and is, a monstrous granite chair.

'Madge Figgy's Chair' is its name, for in it Madge Figgy, who was a wrecker by trade, used to sit and call up the storms, and here, while the rough, cruel Atlantic boiled and lashed in impotent fury over the face of the ladder, Madge sat cool and unconcerned, keeping a sharp look out for any vessels coming in on that terrible coast.

As well as being a wrecker, Madge Figgy was one of the most cruel and wicked witches in the county; and hour after hour she would sit in her chair plotting mischief, or hurling curses at any unfortunate person or thing who had happened to offend her. The poor country-folk were afraid of their very lives of her, and whatever wicked things she told them to do, they had to do them, for they knew her power and lived in terror of offending her.

Amongst the witches she was the leader in all their frolics and revels and wickedness. Getting astride her broomstick she would fly right away across the sea to some foreign land, a band of her friends and cronies after her, and right well did they enjoy themselves,—which was more than anyone else did who came across them while on their wicked revels.

Madge Figgy's home was in a little cottage in a cove not far from her ladder and chair, and this cove was a nest of a gang of the worst wreckers in Cornwall, gathered together by old Madge to help her in her cruel work. No one can count how many noble vessels they lured on to the rocks of that dangerous coast, how many bodies they stripped and cast back into the sea again; while as for the treasure they had divided amongst themselves!— they had quite enough to live on for the rest of their lives, even if they never did another stroke of mischief. That, though, was not what they cared about. They loved wrecking and robbing, and all their evil ways, and would have been quite miserable if they had had to live quiet, respectable stay-at-home lives.

Where all were so wicked there were none to shame them into being any better, and they flaunted their stolen riches as shamelessly as though they had come by everything honestly. It was quite a common sight to see the great, clumsy country-women and girls going about their work dressed in costly silks and velvets, all of the richest character and most beautiful colouring, digging and ploughing, cooking and scrubbing with valuable jewellery on their great arms and their coarse red hands, sparkling gems in their ears, and very likely a tiara that would have made a queen envious, fastened round their untidy, unbrushed hair.

Of all the crew, though, Madge and her husband were the very worst. Most of them did abide by the old saying, 'Honour amongst wreckers,' but not those two. If they could cheat or trick even their friends they would do so; and did, too, very often.

One particularly stormy day, Madge Figgy sat in her great chair in high glee. A tempest such as was seldom known, even on that coast, was raging round her, and close on to the rocks below her was drifting a Portuguese Indiaman which she had lured in to be dashed to fragments on the terrible rocks by the boiling, maddened breakers which towered up like mountains, then broke and fell with all their force on the helpless vessel.

Madge Figgy kicked her heels and clapped her hands with joy as she watched, for the huge vessel laden with valuables of the costliest kind was a prize such as they did not often get, and Madge in her mind was already reckoning up her gains. Far better for the Indiaman had she dropped her treasure overboard and sent it to the bottom of the sea, where she would be ere long; for Madge could tell at any distance what a ship's cargo was worth, and if it was a small one she let the vessel sail on in peace.

Up aloft was the old witch dancing and singing, and down below struggled the perishing crew, captain, sailors, passengers, men, women and children, shrieking aloud for help, but seeing never a living creature coming to give them a hand. Their cries might have melted hearts of iron, but not the hearts of those who were hiding behind the rocks watching with greedy interest for the moment when they might go down and seize their prey. One by one the cries ceased as the sea swallowed up the poor struggling creatures, then presently the vessel broke up, and in on the waves came floating cases, casks, chests, broken spars, mingled with the dead bodies of men and women and little babies.

As fast as they appeared they were seized on, and quickly stripped of everything that was of value, the ladies were robbed of their jewels and dresses, and even of their long hair, and even the babies were robbed of the necklaces which still hung around their chubby necks.

When the bodies were stripped they were not thrown into the sea again, but were carried away and buried in a great green hollow near Perloe Cove, with a stone at the head of each to mark the spot. Though the graves cannot be distinguished now, the hollow may yet be seen.

For weeks after the wreck of the Portuguese Indiaman, the wreckers were continually finding gold and jewels washed in to the sand, and now and again more bodies were washed ashore, all richly dressed. Oh, it was a fine haul the wreckers had after that black storm, but one very curious thing happened such as had never happened before.

Amongst the bodies washed in was that of a beautiful lady, dressed in the richest of robes, and wearing more magnificent jewellery than any of the other poor creatures. In addition to her jewellery, too, she had, fastened about her, a very large amount of money and treasure, as though, poor lady, she had thought that she could not only save herself, but a great deal else as well.

When Madge Figgy, who had claimed this body, had finished stripping it, she stood gazing at it very attentively for a long time. She appeared to be troubled about something, almost frightened, in fact, and turning to the rest of the gang she forbade them to divide any of the spoil, or even to touch a single thing.

There was a fine row at that, of course, for they had all been counting on a rich share, and they vowed they would have it, too! They quarrelled, and fought, and a good deal of blood was spilt, but Madge took care of herself and got the better of them all, too, for it would have taken more than a gang of wreckers to outwit that wicked old woman.

She declared that there was a mark on the body which she understood, though no one else could, and that if they divided any of the things belonging to it, ill-luck would befall them all, and no one knew where it would end.

"Trust a witch to know a witch!" she cried. She got her way, as she generally did, for they were all afraid of her, and everything belonging to the poor lady was put into a chest which stood in Madge's kitchen, while the body was carried to the hollow and buried with the others.

The very night, though, after they had laid her in her grave, a very curious thing happened. Out from the grave there came, as soon as darkness fell, a little blue light. For a moment it flickered and gleamed on the newly made mound, then glided swiftly away up over the cliffs until it reached Madge Figgy's great granite chair. Up into the chair it glided, and there it stayed for a long time, a weird, mysterious gleam, looking most uncanny in the darkness. Then out of the chair it glided and made its way to Madge Figgy's cottage, where it floated across the threshold and straight to the chest where the dead lady's belongings lay.

All the wreckers were watching it, and all, except old Madge, were very nearly terrified out of their senses. They felt sure that at last their wickedness was to meet with its punishment, that the Evil One had come to carry them away, and their hours on earth were numbered.

Madge Figgy tried hard to laugh away their fears and cheer them up. She wanted no 'chicken-hearts' about her, men who would refuse to take part in her wicked work, or even carry tales where she did not want them carried.

"Get along, you great stupids, you!" cried Madge, trying to put some spirit into them, "it will all come right in time. I know all about it!"

It took a long time, though, and the people began to lose faith in Madge's cleverness; for three long months the little blue flame crept out of the dead lady's grave at nightfall, glided to Madge Figgy's chair, and then to the chest in the cottage, and nothing could stop it.

At the end of three months, when the people of the Cove were feeling they could not bear this thing any longer, there came to Madge's cottage one day a curiously dressed stranger. From his appearance all who saw him concluded that he was a foreigner, but from what part of the world he came no one could tell, for never a word escaped his lips.

Madge Figgy's old husband, who was home alone when the stranger arrived, was very nearly scared to death. Firstly because the sight of a stranger always frightened any of that wicked crew, and secondly because of the man's signs and curious gesticulations. Old Figgy thought that he was a madman, sure enough.

After some time, though, and a good many signs and misunderstandings, the old man gathered that the stranger wished to see the graves of the poor souls who went down in the wreck of the Portuguese Indiaman. Old Figgy put on his cap readily enough to show him the way, only too thankful to get him out of the house; but as soon as ever they had started on the right road, the stranger did not need any further guidance, he walked on by himself straight to the hollow, and making his way direct to the grave of the Portuguese lady he threw himself on it passionately, and broke into the most violent outburst of grief imaginable.

For some time old Figgy stood watching him in astonishment, until the foreigner, looking up, caught sight of him, and signed to him to go away; then returning to the grave, again, he threw himself on it once more and stayed there weeping and moaning until nightfall.

When darkness crept on up rose the little blue flame from the grave as before, but, instead of going to Madge Figgy's chair it made its way to the cottage, and gliding on to the chest, gleamed there with twice its usual brilliancy.

The foreigner, who had followed the flame closely, went, without let or hindrance from the old witch or anyone, straight to the chest, and clearing away with one sweep all the rubbish and lumber which were piled on it, opened it as if he had known it all his life, picked out everything in it that had belonged to the lady, then, without touching anything else that the chest contained, closed it again, and, after giving liberal gifts to every wrecker in the place, departed as mysteriously as he had come.

Anything of his history, or whence he came, was never discovered, but from the moment he left Madge Figgy's cottage neither he nor the little blue flame was ever seen again by any of them.

HOW MADGE FIGGY GOT HER PIG.

Madge Figgy, as you already know, spent most of her life in injuring someone. After she had left her cottage by the sea, where she spent so much of her time in robbing the dead, she went to live in St. Buryan, and there she spent her time in robbing the living, and doing any other mischief that came into her head to do.

One of her victims here was her near neighbour, Tom Trenoweth, a hard-working, struggling man who spent all his days trying to make both ends meet, and mostly failing, poor fellow. Now Tom had a sow, a fine great creature, on which he set great store, for when she was fattened up enough he meant to take her to Penzance Market, where he hoped to sell her for at least twenty shillings, for she was worth that and more of any man's money.

As ill-luck would have it, though, Madge Figgy caught sight of the sow one day, and from that moment she could not rest until she had got it for herself.

Over she bustled to Tom's house in a great hurry. "Tom," she said, "I've taken a fancy to that sow of yours, and I'll give 'ee five shillings for her, now this very minute, if you'll sell her. Four would be a good price, but I've set my mind on having her, and I don't mind stretching a point for a friend."

"I ain't going to sell her now," said Tom, "I'm fattening her up for market, and it's a long sight more than five shillings I'm thinking I'll get for her. So keep your money, Madge, you may want it yet," he added meaningly.

"Very well," replied the witch, shaking her finger at Tom, and wagging her head; "I won't press 'ee to sell the pig, but mark my words, before very long you will wish you had!" and away she went without another word.

Poor Tom! He did mark her words, and many a time he remembered them with sorrow, for from the moment they were uttered his sow began to fail. She ate and drank as much as ever he chose to give her, and seemed to enjoy her food, too, but instead of growing fatter she grew leaner and leaner, and from being a fine great beast, nearly fit for a Christmas market, she became a poor, spare-looking thing that no one would say 'thank you' for.

"Are you willing to sell her now, Tom?" cried cruel old Madge, popping her head round the door of the pig-sty one day, when Tom was feeding the animal.

"No, and I wouldn't sell her to you for her weight in gold," cried Tom, too desperate now to care whether he offended the woman or not. "So get home to your own house, you ill-wishing cross-grained old witch!"

Madge Figgy only smiled. "Don't lose your temper, Tom, my dear," she said sweetly, "'tis for me to do that. Just wait a bit, and I'll be bound that before another week is out you'll be glad to get rid of her, even to me!" and away trotted the mischievous old creature, cackling to herself, and rubbing her hands with glee.

"I'll fatten the pig up somehow," cried Tom desperately, and he began giving her more than double her usual quantity of food at each meal. He gave her enough, indeed, to fatten two pigs, and nearly ruined himself to do it; but the more she ate the thinner she grew, and before the week was out she was merely skin and bone. "I can't afford to spend no more on 'ee," said Tom sorrowfully, and he made up his mind to take her to market the very next day before she got any worse.

So, early the following morning they started off to walk to the market. Tom tied a string around the sow's leg to prevent her running away, but there was little enough fear of her doing that, for the poor thing could scarcely stand for weakness. In fact, she kept on falling down from sheer inability to support herself, and Tom had to pick her up and put her on her feet again, for she had not got the strength to get up by herself.

After a long time, for they only went at a snail's pace, they came to the high road. "I believe I'll have to take and carry her on my back," said Tom dolefully, "or we shan't get to market till night." But hardly had he spoken the words when the sow took to her heels, and ran as if she had been a stag with the hounds after her!

Poor Tom was nearly shaken to bits, and his arms were pretty nearly dragged from his body, for over hedges and ditches she went, and over everything else that came in her way, dragging Tom after her, until at last he had to drop the rope and let her take her chance, for his strength was all gone, and he had no breath left.

As soon, though, as Tom let go his hold of the rope, the creature stopped her mad race, and walked along as quietly and soberly as the best-behaved pig that ever breathed. She went, though, every way but the right one, and this she did for mile upon mile, taking Tom after her, until at last they came to Tregenebris Downs.

Here, where the two roads branch off, the one to Sancreed and the other to Penzance, Tom caught hold of the rope again, and tried once more to lead her to market, but the moment she came to the cross-roads, the sow started off at full speed again, jerking the rope out of Tom's hand, and careering away by herself until she got under Tregenebris Bridge. Here, though, she was forced to stop, for she stuck fast, and could not move backwards or forwards, for Tregenebris Bridge was a queer, old-fashioned construction, more like a big drain-pipe than anything, except that it was smaller in the middle than at the ends. Consequently, as she could not go through it and come out the other side, and she would not come back, she had to stay where she was.

Tom did not know what to do. He could not reach her to pull her out, and all his holloaing and shouting was so much waste of breath. He pelted her with stones and lumps of turf, first her head and then her tail, until he was tired, but he might just as well have left her, for all the good it did. She only grunted, and planted her feet more obstinately.

At last Tom, being quite worn out, sat down to rest, and waited to see what she would do if left to herself, but though he waited and waited till evening, the pig never budged. Tom, though, grew so hungry that he hardly knew how to bear with himself. He had had nothing to eat or drink since five in the morning, and he had tramped miles upon miles since that time.

"There don't seem much chance of the contrairy old thing's coming out, so I may as well go home to get some supper," he said at last. "If anybody finds her they'll know she's mine, for there isn't such another poor miserable creature in the parish. So here goes." But no sooner had he made a start than whom should he see coming towards him but Madge Figgy.

Madge was smiling to herself as she walked along, as though she were very well pleased about something. "Hulloa, Tom Trenoweth!" she cried, pretending to be surprised. "What are you doing here?"

"Well," said Tom, "that's more than I can tell you, but I ain't here for my own pleasure, I can assure you of that, and if you want to know more you can look under the bridge and find out for yourself."

"What's that grunting in there? Surely never your old sow! Well, she can't have fattened much if she's got in there! Are you in the mind to part with her now, Tom? What will you let me have her for now?"

"If you've got a bit of something to eat in your basket, for pity's sake let me have it, for I'm famished; and if you can get the old thing out of that there pipe you're welcome to her for your trouble," said Tom sullenly, for he felt small at giving in to his enemy after all.

"I've got a beautiful new kettle loaf in my basket, Tom; take it and welcome, do."

Tom seized the loaf and began to eat ravenously. "Thank 'ee," said he, pretending to smile. "I think I've got the best of that bargain, for anyway I've got a good loaf, and it'll take more than you to get out my old pig!"

"Ha, ha!" laughed Madge Figgy, "I'm glad you are pleased, Tom, ha, ha! refused five shillings, and took a twopenny loaf! I'm pleased with my share of the bargain, and I'm glad you are." Then turning towards the pig she called softly, "Chug! chug! chug! Come on, chug! chug! chug!"

Out walked the old sow at once, and going up to the witch, she trotted away down the road after her as tamely as a dog.

THE STORY OF SIR TRISTRAM AND LA BELLE ISEULT.

Long, long ago, when Arthur was King of England, and King Mark was King of Cornwall,—for there were many petty kings, who held their lands under King Arthur,—there was born in Lyonesse a little boy, a king's son.

Instead, though, of there being great joy and rejoicing at the birth of the little heir, sorrow reigned throughout Lyonesse, for his father, King Melodias, had been stolen away by enchantment, no one knew where. Nor could anyone tell how to release him, and the heartbroken queen was dying of grief, for she loved her husband very dearly.

When she saw her little son her tears fell fast on his baby face. "Call him Tristram," she said, "for he was born in sorrow," and as she spoke she fell back dead.

Little Tristram wailed right lustily, as though he fully realized his orphan state, and wept with pity for his own sad fate; and good cause he had to wail, too, poor little man, had he but known it, for already the greedy barons had cast their eyes on his land, longing to possess it and rule it. With only a baby boy standing between them and it, their way was easy enough. His death could easily be accomplished.

Fortunately, though, for him, and everyone else in the land, King Melodias was just then released from enchantment by Merlin the wizard, and came hurrying joyfully to his home, to embrace his beloved wife. Great was his grief when he found that she was dead, great was the moan he made in his sorrow. With great pomp and splendour he buried her, and for seven years lived a lonely life, mourning her.

At the end of that time he married again, but the stepmother hated little Tristram, the heir, and longed to destroy him, that her own child might be king. So one day she placed some poison in a cup for him to drink, but her own child, being thirsty, drank the poison and died.

The queen, broken-hearted at the loss of her boy, and horror-stricken at what she had done, hated her stepson more than ever after this, and once again she tried to kill him in the same manner. This time, though, King Melodias, spying the tempting-looking drink, took it up and was about to drink it, when the queen, seeing what he was about to do, rushed in and snatched it from him. Then he discovered her guilt, and his anger knew no bounds.

"Thou traitress!" he cried, "confess what manner of drink this is, or here and now I will run this sword through thy heart!"

So she confessed, and was tried before the barons, and by their judgment was given over to be burnt to death. The faggots were prepared, the queen was bound to the stake, and they were beginning to light the fire when little Tristram, flinging himself on his knees, besought his father with such entreaties to pardon her, that the king could not refuse. So the queen was released, and in time the king forgave her.

But, though he forgave her, he could never trust her again, and to protect little Tristram from her, he was sent to France, where he continued for some time, learning to joust and hunt, and do all things that were right and brave and noble; and seven years passed before he returned to his home in Lyonesse.

Lyonesse was the furthest point of Cornwall; it joined what we now call 'Land's End,' and stretched out through the sea until it reached the Scilly Islands, a wild, rugged, beautiful spot, washed on either side by the glorious Atlantic sea. One day, though, that glorious Atlantic rose like a mountain above Lyonesse, and where in the morning had been a beautiful city with churches and houses, and fertile lands, in the evening there was only a raging, boiling sea, bearing on its bosom fragments of the lost world it had devoured. This, though, was long after the time of which I am writing now.

For two years after his return from France, Tristram lived in Lyonesse, and then it happened that King Anguish of Ireland sent to King Mark of Cornwall to demand seven years' truage that was due to him. But when the demand reached King Mark, he and his knights absolutely refused to pay the money, and sent the messenger back, with none too polite a message, to say so. If he wanted the debt settled, they said, he could send the noblest knight of his court to fight for it, otherwise the king might whistle for his money.

King Anguish was furiously enraged when this message reached him, and calling to him at once Sir Marhaus, his biggest and trustiest knight, sent him without delay to Cornwall to fight this battle.

So Sir Marhaus set sail, and King Mark was troubled when he heard who was coming against him, for he knew well he had no knight to match him.

At last Sir Marhaus arrived, but he did not land at once; for seven days he abode in his ship, and each day he sent to King Mark a stern demand for the money.

The king had no intention of paying the money, but he sorely wanted a knight to fight for him. One worthy by birth and skill to meet this great champion; and in great ado he sent all over the country in search of such a one. At last, when none was to be found at home, someone counselled the king to send to King Arthur at Camelot for one of the Knights of the Round Table; but that could not be, for Sir Marhaus himself was a Round Table knight, and they, of course, never fought each other, unless it was in private quarrel.

When at last the news of all this reached young Tristram's ears, he felt very greatly mortified that there could not be found in Cornwall a knight to fight for their rights, and his heart burned within him to go and save the honour of the West Country. He went to his father, King Melodias. "It seems to me," he cried impetuously, "a shame to us all, that Sir Marhaus, who is brother to the Queen of Ireland, should go back and say we Cornishmen have no one worthy to fight him."

"Alas," answered the king, "know ye not that Sir Marhaus is one of the noblest of Arthur's knights, the best knights of the world? Beyond those of the Table Round I know none fit to match him."

"Then," cried Tristram, "I would I were a knight, for if Sir Marhaus departs to Ireland unscathed, I will never more hold up my head for very shame. Sir, give me leave to go to my uncle, King Mark, that I may by him be made a knight."

King Melodias could deny his son nothing, so, "Do as your courage bids you," he said, and Tristram, filled with joy, rode away at once to his uncle's court, and as soon as he arrived there he heard nothing but great dole made that no one could be found to fight the Irish knight.

"Who are you?" asked the king, when Tristram presented himself before him, "and whence come you?" he added, looking admiringly at the handsome stranger.

"Sir, I am Tristram of Lyonesse; I come from King Melodias, whose son I am; my mother was your sister."

Then King Mark rejoiced greatly, for he saw in this stalwart nephew a champion for Cornwall, and, having knighted him, he sent word to Sir Marhaus to say he had found a champion to do battle with him.

"I shall fight with none but of the blood-royal," Sir Marhaus sent back word; "your champion must be either a king's son or a queen's."

Whereupon King Mark sent word to say that his champion was better born than ever Sir Marhaus was, and that his name was Tristram of Lyonesse, whose father was a king, and his mother a queen, and a king's sister.

So it was arranged that the fight should take place on an island near, and thither Sir Tristram went in a ship with his horse, and his man Gouvernail, and all that he could need. And so noble he looked, and so brave, and of so good heart, that not one who saw him depart could refrain from weeping, for they never thought to see him return alive.

So, on the island those two noble knights met, and Sir Marhaus was sad to see one so young and well-favoured come against him. "I sore repent," said he, "of your courage, for hear me that against all the noblest and trustiest knights of the world have I been matched and never yet been beaten. So take my counsel, and return again to your ship while you are able."

"Sir," said Sir Tristram, throwing up his head proudly, "I have been made a knight that I might come against you, and I have sworn never to leave you until you are conquered or I am dead, for I will fight to the death to rescue Cornwall from the old truage."

So they lowered their spears, and without more ado the fight began, and such a fight as that was never seen or known before in Cornwall. At the very first charge they met with such force that Sir Marhaus's spear wounded Sir Tristram in the side, and horses and riders were sent rolling on the ground; but soon they were on their feet again, and freeing themselves of their horses and spears, they pulled out their shields and fought with swords. With their swords they slashed and smote each other until the blood poured from them in streams, and so courageous were they, and determined not to give in, that they fought on and on until it seemed as though that struggle would last for ever. They hurled at each other with such fury that the blood ran down them in streams, dyeing the ground all round, yet neither prevailed in the least degree.

By and by, though, Sir Tristram, being the younger and the better-winded, proved the fresher, and drawing up all his strength for one last effort, he smote Sir Marhaus on the helm with such force that Sir Marhaus fell on his knees, and the sword cleaving through helmet and skull stuck so fast in the bone that Sir Tristram had to pull three times at it with all his might before he could get it free, and when it did come, a piece of the edge of the sword was left behind in the skull.

Overcome with pain and shame at his defeat, Sir Marhaus with a mighty effort raised himself to his feet, and without speaking one word, flung from him his sword and his shield, and staggered away to his ship.

"Ah!" mocked Sir Tristram, "why do you, a knight of the Table Round, flee from a knight so young and untried as I?" But Sir Marhaus made as though he did not hear the taunts, but hurrying on board his ship, set sail with all possible speed.

"Well, Sir Knight," laughed Tristram, "I thank you for your sword and shield; I will keep them wherever I go, and the shield I will carry to the day of my death." So Sir Marhaus returned to Ireland, and there, in spite of all that physicians could do, he soon died of his disgrace and his wounds; and after he was dead, the piece of sword-blade, which could not be extracted before, was found embedded in his brainpan.

When the queen, his sister, saw the piece of sword-blade which was taken from her brother's skull, she asked that she might have it; and putting it away in a secret spot she vowed a solemn vow that when she had found out who had done this thing, she would never rest until she had had revenge.

But about that time Sir Tristram, who had been severely wounded himself, was also lying at the point of death, neither knowing nor caring to know of the blessings and praises showered upon him; and great was the grief that filled the hearts of all the leeches and surgeons for whom King Mark had sent, for not one was of any avail, and the gallant young knight who had saved the honour of Cornwall was more than like to die.

At last, when hope was well-nigh dead, there came a lady to the court who told King Mark that his nephew would never recover from his wounds unless he went to the land whence the poisoned spear came, for there only could he be healed.

So, with all speed was a vessel prepared, and on board it Sir Tristram was carried, and with his man Gouvernail, his dogs, his horses, and his harp, he sailed until he came to Ireland. Here they all landed, and Sir Tristram was borne carefully on shore, to a castle prepared for him, where he was laid on a bed, and there on his bed he lay day after day, playing on his harp so exquisitely that all the people crowded to listen to him, for such music had never been heard in that country before.

By and by the news of the presence of this wonderful player was carried to the king and queen, who were dwelling not very far away: and the king and queen sent for him to come to them; but when they found that he was a wounded knight, they had him brought to the castle, and there his wound was dressed and every care taken of him, for now they all grew to have a great admiration and liking for him. But who he was, or where he came from, they had no idea, for he had not told anyone his real name, or the story of the joust in which he got his wound.

Now in all that land there was no better surgeon than the king's own daughter, the lady Iseult,—who, because of her loveliness, was known as La Belle Iseult.—So presently the king, who came to feel a greater and greater liking for Sir Tristram, and was anxious to see him well again, gave him over to the charge of his daughter, in whose skill he had great faith; for none other seemed able to heal him.

So La Belle Iseult nursed him, and attended to his wound, and soon, at the bottom of it, she found the poison, which she removed, and quickly healed him. Before this end was reached, though, Sir Tristram had grown to love his beautiful nurse, and she her patient; for La Belle

Iseult with her flower-like face and large grey eyes, her broad, low brow, round which her gleaming golden hair waved softly, and fell in heavy waves to her knees, was wondrously lovable. And Sir Tristram was more than passing noble, and his manners were gentle and courteous. When he grew stronger he taught Iseult to play the harp, and they sang songs together, so that they saw much of one another.

Someone else loved Iseult also, and this was Sir Palamides the Saracen, and many fair gifts he brought the lady to win her love. But ladies are not to be won thus, and Iseult did not love the Saracen knight. Indeed, she besought Sir Tristram to joust with him and conquer him, that she might be rid of him, both of which Sir Tristram did, though Sir Palamides had put to the worse many brave knights before, and most men were afraid of him. Sir Tristram, whom Iseult had arrayed in white harness, rode against him on a white horse and threw him, and Sir Palamides was sore ashamed and would have crept secretly from the field, and from the crowds of knights and ladies watching the jousts, had not Sir Tristram gone after him and bid him return and finish the joust. So Palamides returned and fought again, but once more Sir Tristram overthrew him, and this time wounded him so sore that he was at his mercy.

"Now," said Sir Tristram, "swear to me that you will do as I command, or I will slay you outright." Sir Palamides seeing his stern face, and remembering his strength, promised. "Then," said Sir Tristram, "promise never more to come near the lady La Belle Iseult, also that for a twelvemonth and a day you will bear no armour, nor wear any harness of war."

"Alas," cried Sir Palamides, "I shall be for ever ashamed and disgraced," but he had to promise, and in fierce vexation he cut to pieces the harness he then wore, and threw the pieces from him. No one but La Belle Iseult knew who the knight was who had jousted with the Saracen, until some time after; and when it was known, Sir Tristram was loved more than ever by the king and queen, as he was already by their daughter.

So month after month Sir Tristram lingered on in Ireland, and did many a noble deed during that time, and there he might have gone on living to the end of the chapter, if it had not been for a sore mischance which befell thus.

One day, while Sir Tristram was absent, the queen and the lady Iseult were wandering up and down his room, when the queen suddenly espied Sir Tristram's sword lying on a couch, and seeing it to be of fine workmanship and delicately wrought, she lifted it the better to examine it, and she and Iseult stood admiring it together. Then presently the queen drew the sword slowly from out its scabbard, and there, within an inch and a half of the point, she espied the broken edge of the blade.

Thrusting the weapon into Iseult's hands she ran to her chamber, where she had, safely locked away, the piece of steel which had been taken from her brother's skull; and bringing it back fitted it to the broken blade exactly.

At that her anger knew no bounds, nor her mortification that they should have treated so well, and grown to love, the slayer of her brother. Sir Tristram happening to return at that moment, her anger so overmastered her that, seizing the sword, she rushed on him and would have slain him there and then, had not Gouvernail caught her and wrested the weapon from her.

Being frustrated she ran in a frenzy of hate to her husband. "My lord," she cried, "we have here, in our very home, the destroyer and slayer of my brother, your most noble and trusty knight."

"Who is he?" cried King Anguish, springing to his feet, "and where?"

"Sir, it is this same knight whom your daughter has healed, and whom we have loved and treated well. I beseech you have no mercy on him, for he deserves none."

"Alas, alas," cried the king, "I am right sorry, for he is as noble a knight as ever I saw. Do him no violence. Leave him to me, and I will deal with him according to my best judgment."

So the king, who loved Sir Tristram, and could not bring himself to have him slain, went to Tristram's chamber, and there he saw him dressed, and ready to mount his horse. Then and there the king told him all that he had learnt, and said, "I love you too well to do you harm, therefore I give you leave to quit this court on one condition, that you tell me your real name, and if you really slew my brother-in-law, Sir Marhaus."

So Tristram told him all his story, and then took leave of the king and all the court; and great was the grief at his departure, but by far the saddest leave-taking was that between him and La Belle Iseult, for they loved each other very dearly. And when they parted Sir Tristram swore to be ever her true and faithful knight, and she, that for seven years she would marry no one else, unless by his consent or desire. Then each gave the other a ring, and with a last long kiss they parted.

So Sir Tristram returned at last to Cornwall, and there stayed with his uncle Mark, at Tintagel, and great were the rejoicings that he had returned recovered of his wound, and stronger and more noble-looking than ever.

When, though, he had been back a little time, a great quarrel arose between King Mark and his nephew, and their feelings grew very hot and angry towards one another. It was about a beautiful lady that they quarrelled, a lady whom King Mark loved more than passing well. He thought that Sir Tristram loved her too, and she him, and he was so jealous of Sir Tristram that one day he and his knights, disguised, rode after him to see if he had gone to meet her. And as Tristram came riding back King Mark bore down on him, and they fought until the king was so wounded that he lay on the ground as though dead, and Sir Tristram rode on his way. He never knew that it was his uncle with whom he had fought, but from that day to the day of his death, though they were fair-spoken to each other, the king never forgave his nephew or loved him again.

Indeed, he hated him so much that he ever plotted to injure him, and at last one day he thought of a plan by which he could ruin Tristram's happiness, and probably get him killed as well.

Now it happened that when Sir Tristram had first returned from Ireland he had told his uncle of La Belle Iseult, of her beauty, and grace, and skill; for his heart was ever filled with love and admiration for her, and to him she was the very fairest woman in the world. So to wound Sir Tristram, and to take a sore and cruel revenge upon him, King Mark determined to ask her in marriage for himself, and to make his cruelty the greater, he determined that Sir Tristram should be the knight who should go to Ireland as his ambassador to ask her hand of King Anguish, her father.

Sending for Sir Tristram he laid his commands upon him, rejoicing in the heavy task he was laying upon him, watching him closely to note how he would bear it. But Sir Tristram, though sad at heart and deeply troubled, bore himself bravely, and accepted the task; for to have refused it would have been a cowardice and a shame, and not the conduct of a true knight.

Without delay he set about preparing for his sad journey. He had made ready a large vessel, fitted in the most sumptuous manner possible, and taking with him some chosen knights dressed in the most goodly style, he set sail from Tintagel for Ireland. Before they had got far, though, a fierce storm burst over them, and beat their vessel about until she was driven back to England, to the coast of Camelot, where King Arthur dwelt, and right glad they were to take to the land.

There, when they were landed, Sir Tristram set up his tent, and hanging his shield without it, lay down to rest. Hardly, though, was he lain down, before two knights of the Round Table, Sir Ector de Maris and Sir Morganor, came and rapped on the shield, bidding him come forth and joust.

"Wait awhile," called back Sir Tristram, "and I will bring you my answer." Then he hastily dressed himself, and came out to the two impatient knights, and without much ado he first smote down Sir Ector and then Sir Morganor, with the same spear.

"Whence come you, and whose knight are you?" they asked as they lay on the ground, unable to rise because of their bruises.

"My lords," answered Sir Tristram, "I am from Cornwall."

"Alas, alas, I am sore ashamed that any Cornish knight should have overcome me," cried Sir Ector. And so ashamed was he that he put off his armour and went away on foot, for he would not ride.

Now it happened about this time that King Anguish of Ireland was sent for to appear at King Arthur's court at Camelot, to answer a charge of treason brought against him by Sir Blamor de Ganis, and Sir Bleoberis, his brother; which was that he had slain at his court a cousin of theirs and of Sir Launcelot.

The king, who had not known for why he was sent, was sore abashed when he heard the charge, for he knew there were only two ways to settle the matter, either he must fight the accuser himself, or he must get a knight to do so for him, and very heavy-hearted he was, for Sir Blamor was a powerful knight, and one of the trustiest of the Table Round, and King Anguish knew that now Sir Marhaus was dead he had no knight in Ireland to match him.

Three days he had in which to decide upon his answer, and great was his perplexity as to what it should be.

Meanwhile, Gouvernail went unto his master and told him that King Anguish was arraigned for murder, and was in great distress. Whereupon Sir Tristram replied, "This is the best news I have heard these seven years, that the King of Ireland hath need of my help. I dare be sworn there is no knight in England, save of Arthur's court, that dare do battle with Sir Blamor de Ganis. Bring me to the king then, Gouvernail, for to win his love I will take this battle on myself."

So Gouvernail went to King Anguish, and told him that a knight wished to do him service. "What knight?" said he.

"Sir Tristram of Lyonesse," answered Gouvernail, "who, for your goodness to him in your own land, would fain assist you in this."

Then was the king right overjoyed, and went unto Sir Tristram's pavilion, and when Sir Tristram saw him he would have knelt and held his stirrup for him to dismount, but the king leapt lightly to the ground, and they embraced each other with great gladness, and the king told his tale.

"Sir," said Sir Tristram, "for your good grace to me, and for the sake of your daughter, Belle Iseult, I will fight this battle, but you must grant me two requests. The first is, you must give me your own word that you were not consenting unto this knight's death; the second, that if I win this battle you shall give me as reward whatsoever reasonable thing I ask." Whereupon the king swore to both of them, and then went to tell his accusers that he had a knight ready to fight Sir Blamor. Then King Arthur commanded Sir Tristram and Sir Blamor to appear before the judges, and when they came many kings and knights who were present recognized Sir Tristram as the young unknown knight who had fought and conquered Sir Marhaus of Ireland, and the excitement grew intense, for two lustier knights than Sir Tristram and Sir Blamor could not have been found.

So the time was fixed, and the combatants retired to their tents to prepare for battle.

"Dear brother," said Bleoberis to Blamor, "remember of what kin you are, and how Sir Launcelot is our cousin, and suffer death rather than shame, for none of our blood was yet shamed in battle."

"Fear not," answered Sir Blamor stoutly, "that I will ever disgrace our kin. Yonder knight is a goodly man, but I swear I will never yield, nor say the loth word. He may smite me down by his chivalry, but he shall slay me before I say the loth word."

So the two champions rode to meet each other from opposite sides of the lists, and they feutred their spears and charged each other with so great force that it sounded as though the heavens were sending forth loud thunders, and then Sir Tristram by his great strength bore Sir Blamor to the ground, and his horse under him.

He was quickly clear of his horse, though, and on his feet again. "Alight, Sir Tristram," he cried, pulling out his sword, "my horse has failed me, but the earth shall not."

So together they rushed, and lashed at each other in fury, slashing and tearing, foining, and making such fearful strokes that the kings and knights held their breath in horror and amazement that two men could use each other so, and neither give in. But so fierce were they that their stabs and cuts might have been falling on men of wood, so little heed did they pay. So fast and furiously they fought, that the wonder was they had breath to keep on; but Sir Blamor was the more furious, and therefore the less wary, so that by and by Sir Tristram saw an opportunity and smote him such a crushing blow on the head that he fell over on his side, and Sir Tristram stood over him.

Then was Sir Blamor's shame piteous. "Kill me, Sir Tristram," he cried, "as you are a noble knight, for I would not live. Not to be lord of the whole universe would I endure with shame; and I will never say the loth word, so the victory is not yours unless you slay me."

Sir Tristram was sore perplexed what to do. He could not bring himself to kill this noble knight; but for his party's sake he must, unless Sir Blamor would say the loth word. So he went to the assembled kings, and kneeling before them he besought them that they would take the matter into their hands. "For," said he, "it is a cruel pity that such a noble knight should be slain, and I pray God he may not be slain or shamed by me. I beseech the king, whose champion I am, that he will have mercy upon this good knight."

Sir Bleoberis, though, as hotly demanded that his brother should be slain outright, until the judges gave him stern reproof.

"It shall not be," they said, "both King Anguish and his champion knight have more mercy than thou," and they went to King Anguish, and he, good man, gave up his claim, and resigned the loth word, as each champion was proved of good faith. And so it was settled, and so rejoiced were Sir Bleoberis and his brother, and right grateful for their goodness, that they swore eternal friendship to King Anguish and Sir Tristram, and each kissed the other, and swore a vow that neither would come against the other in combat.

Then King Anguish and Sir Tristram set sail for Ireland, with great splendour and gladness, and right welcome was Sir Tristram when the people heard what he had done for their king and for them. Great were the rejoicings, and great the joy, but the joy of Iseult was greater than all the rest together, for she still loved Sir Tristram with all her heart and soul. Then as the days came and went, much did King Anguish marvel that Sir Tristram had not made his second request, but Sir Tristram was fain to postpone doing so, for he was heavy-hearted at his task. At last King Anguish asked him, saying, "Sir Knight, you have not yet asked of me your reward."

"Alas," said Sir Tristram sadly, "the time is come. I would ask you for your daughter Iseult to take back with me to Cornwall,—not for myself, but to wed the king, my uncle Mark; for full well he knows how she surpasseth all in beauty, and wisdom, and charm, for I myself have told him of her, until he desireth her greatly for his queen and lady."

"Ah me!" cried King Anguish in amazement, and, "Ah me!" he sighed, "I would you had asked her for yourself, Sir Tristram. Right glad would I have been to have called you 'son!'"

"That can never be now," said Sir Tristram gently; "I should be false to my trust, and for ever shamed. My uncle commanded me to come, and I have promised."

So a great feasting and merry-making began, and all things were made ready for La Belle Iseult to sail to another land to be made a queen. Now whether the queen, Iseult's mother, saw that Sir Tristram and her daughter loved each other, or whether she feared that her daughter might not love King Mark, no one will ever know, but she set to work to concoct a love-drink, brewing it from delicate herbs and simples, which when ready she enclosed in a golden flask. This she handed to Dame Bragwaine, La Belle Iseult's waiting-woman, bidding her guard it with all care, and not let it out of her sight until La Belle Iseult and King Mark were wedded, when she was to give it to them that they might each drink of it, so that a great and holy love should rise and grow between them, never to die until their lives ended.

So, on a certain day a dainty vessel, all painted white and silver, and furnished with the utmost richness and beauty, set sail from Ireland. At the prow glittered a golden swallow, all set with gems, and on board were Tristram and Iseult.

Silently, swiftly they glided through the waters, the sun shone softly, the breeze lightly caressed the dainty, bird-like vessel and the white fluttering canvas, as though afraid to breathe on anything so lovely as the lady lying amidst her silken cushions and cloth of gold. Then it stole modestly away, only to return again, full fain to touch her golden hair, or her delicate cheek. The scent of the land-flowers filled the air, for the vessel was gaily bedecked with all the fairest and most delicate.

In this little nest of luxury sat Tristram and Iseult, he so stalwart, noble, bronzed, she so surpassingly beautiful, gentle and lovable. All through the long, warm days they sat listening each to the other's talk, and when the sun went down and left them to the fair white light of the moon, they still sat and talked, or looked at each other, for the mere sight of each filled the other's heart with joy.

Oh the pity of it all! the pity of it! Such a nobly-matched pair was never seen before nor since.

Iseult made Sir Tristram tell her of the battles he had fought, of the countries he had seen, and of the people of this new land towards which she was hastening; for all was strange to her, and a great heaviness filled her heart at the thought of King Mark and his court.

That her mind might not dwell on it, she asked him of Queen Guinevere, the fame of whose beauty had spread to all lands.

"Alas, alas for her beauty!" cried Sir Tristram. "It has been the undoing of many good men and true, who have died for love of her. Her beauty has been a sore curse to her, poor lady."

"Then," answered Iseult, looking up at him with serious, innocent eyes, "right thankful I am that my face will never bring ill-fortune to any man!" And Sir Tristram had to turn from her to hide his pain, for his love for her was greater than ever.

On and on they sailed, full fain that their voyage might last as long as might be, for perfect was their happiness to be together thus, and everything was fair and peaceful. But at last one day the sun was hid by the clouds which gathered in the sky above them, the wind howled threateningly around the vessel, increasing in violence as the hours dragged by, until the danger of the dainty craft was great.

Ill indeed would it have been with them but for the might of Sir Tristram's arm, for the vessel was not one built to battle with tempests and mighty seas. With all his strength and skill he guided her through the troubled waters, and Iseult sat and watched him at his task, marvelling at his power. "Ah," she thought, "had I been a man I would have been just like to him." And, without fear of danger, so perfectly did she trust in him, she lay and gazed at him with admiring, wistful eyes. From time to time he came to her to encourage and reassure her, but although she felt no fear, she did not tell him so, so dearly did she love to hear his voice, and feel his care for her.

At last when the danger was over he came to her again, dropping beside her almost exhausted. "Iseult, my throat is parched and burning, my tongue cleaves to my mouth. Give me some drink," he pleaded.

Pleased to do his bidding, glad to be able to help him, Iseult rose and ran below. But in the confusion caused by the storm nowhere could she find aught wherewith to quench his thirst. Dame Bragwaine, half dead with terror of the storm, fatigue, and sickness, lay in a sort of stupor on her couch, and Iseult, ever kind and thoughtful for others, would not disturb her to help her in her search. Here and there she sought, and high and low, but nowhere could she find wine or aught else to drink.

Right vexed and disappointed, she was returning empty-handed to the deck where Sir Tristram impatiently awaited her, when, close by the couch of Dame Bragwaine, she spied a beautiful golden flask full of a rich sparkling liquid. With a cry of relief she snatched it up, and running up on deck, "Drink, drink," she cried, unloosing the fastening, "the perfume is intoxicating. Such wine I never before beheld."

"Nay, sweet Lady Iseult," cried Sir Tristram, pressing it back into her hands; "deign first to put your lips to it; do me that honour, or I will never taste it." So to her sweet parted lips she raised the flask, and drank, and then, smiling and glad, she handed it to him.

Alas, alas, unhappy pair, who might have been so happy! No sooner had they tasted of that fatal drink than through their hearts and brains poured a love so great, so deep, so surpassing, that never a greater could exist in this world. And in their hearts it dwelt for evermore, never leaving them through weal or woe.

At last, alas, after many adventures and many dangers, the happy voyage ended, the coast of Cornwall was reached, and Sir Tristram had to lead La Belle Iseult to the king. And King Mark when he saw her was so amazed at her beauty that he loved her there and then, and with great pomp and rejoicing the marriage took place at once.

But La Belle Iseult loved none but Sir Tristram, and he her.

For a while all went well, but only for a little while, for King Mark, told by his knights of the love Queen Iseult and Sir Tristram bore each other, grew sore jealous of Sir Tristram, and hating him more and more, longed for a chance to do him harm.

But Tristram gave him no chance, for he was the noblest and trustiest knight of all the court, and though he fought and jousted continually no harm came to him until one unhappy day, when he was lying sleeping in a wood, there came along, a man whose brother Sir Tristram had killed; when the man saw Sir Tristram lying there asleep he shot an arrow at him, and the arrow went through Tristram's shoulder.

Sir Tristram was on his feet in a moment, and killed the man; but his own hurt was a grievous one, for the arrow had been a poisoned one, so, what with his poisoned wound and what with his sorrow that Iseult was so kept a prisoner by King Mark, that he could neither see her nor hear from her, he was very ill for a long time, and like to die. And no one had the skill to cure him but La Belle Iseult, and she might not do so.

Hearing, though, by some means, of his sad condition she sent to him a message by Dame Bragwaine's cousin, bidding him to go to Brittany, for King Howell's daughter, Iseult la Blanche Mains,—or Iseult of the White Hands,—could cure him, and no one else. So he took a ship and went, and this other Iseult healed his wounds, and restored him to perfect health. But she grew to love him, too, for he was a man to whom all women's hearts softened.

She was but a child, this White-handed Iseult. She had barely reached her sixteenth year. And though she thought of her unasked love with shame, and though she ever strove to hide it, it shone in her soft brown eyes, and pale face, and filled Sir Tristram's heart with pain for her. So he left the court and sailed the seas again, hoping that she would forget him, and learn to love someone else.

Now, though Sir Tristram could not tear the love of La Belle Iseult from his heart, he did not spend his life in moans and sad regrets. He gave his life to helping the oppressed, and destroying the oppressors; to helping to right wrongs, and in all ways living a good and noble life worthy of the lady who loved him.

His liking for the sea was great, too, so that he spent many days and nights on board his own good ship, and often he thought of the time when La Belle Iseult crossed the sea with him, of the sunny days and starry nights, the peace, the joy, and the happiness of that sweet time. And his heart ached cruelly, and he was full of sadness, for he was a very lonely man now, with no hope of happiness before him.

Then one day in his loneliness came the thought of that other lonely heart,—kind little Iseult of the White Hands, and of her love for him. "She suffers as I do," he said. "Why should two women suffer so for my sake? I cannot love her as she deserves, but I will try to make her happy." So, turning the vessel's head, he made once more for Brittany, and there he found that an earl called Grip was making great war upon King Howell, and was getting the mastery. So Sir Tristram joyfully went to the king's aid, and after mowing down Grip's knights right and left, he killed the earl himself, and so won the battle.

Right royally was Sir Tristram received after that, and King Howell in his joy would have given him his whole kingdom had he so desired. But Sir Tristram would accept no reward. What he had done, was done for Iseult's sake, he said. And a love grew up in Tristram's heart for the gentle maiden, for who could help loving one kind and beautiful!

So they were married with great rejoicings, and all the kingdom was glad, and so was Sir Tristram, for now, he thought, he could quench that fatal love for Iseult of Cornwall, and could spend the rest of his days in this sunny land, happy with his sweet child-wife.

Alas! alas! Once more the deadly love-drink did its work! No sooner had he placed the ring on his bride's finger, than the love for the other Iseult returned stronger than ever.

"I have been false to my lady!" he cried to himself remorsefully, "for I swore ever to be her true knight, loyal to her alone." And such sorrow and repentance filled his heart that his love for his bride was killed. He concealed his pain so well, though, that little Iseult was happy, never doubting that her husband loved her,—but all the days and nights that passed were full for Tristram of yearning for his love, and a great longing to be again in Cornwall.

At last one day there arrived at the castle a knight from King Arthur's court at Camelot; and of him Sir Tristram asked, "Say they aught of me at court?"

"Truly," answered the knight, "they speak of you with shame, for Sir Launcelot says you are a false knight to your lady, and his love for you is dead, so that he longs to meet with you that he may joust with you."

Sore troubled indeed was Sir Tristram at this, for he loved Sir Launcelot, and coveted his respect, and to be deemed traitor to the lady for whom he would have laid down his life, hurt him most of all.

From that time his longing to return to Tintagel and his love for La Belle Iseult grew daily more and more unconquerable, until at last he could no longer bear it, and one day set sail from Brittany, leaving his poor little lonely wife behind to mourn his absence, and yearn for his return; for as yet she had not found out that there was no love at all in his heart for her.

But on a day soon after he had left her there was brought to her the story of his love for that other Iseult, and of hers for him. Then was the young wife filled with shame that ever she had showed her love for him, and jealousy raged in her, turning her love to bitter hate, and her heart hardened so that night and day she longed to be revenged.

Thus a whole year passed away, and Tristram and Queen Iseult loved each other as dearly as ever; but King Mark in his jealous anger kept them so watched that they could never see or speak one to the other, and they had no peace or joy in life, until at last they could bear the pain no longer, and one day they managed to escape together and to reach the Castle of Joyous Gard, where the king had no power to reach them, even had he known where they were hid. Of their love and happiness there no tongue can tell, and of the peace and joy of their life, for they loved each other above all else, and when they were together nothing had power to pain them.

But at last, on a sad, sad day, the trusty Gouvernail came to Sir Tristram with word that a summons had been sent him from King Arthur, to go to the aid of Sir Triamour of Wales, for he was sore beset by a monster named Urgan, and needed help.

Sir Tristram could in no wise, of course, neglect this summons, for that would have been the direst disgrace to him, and never more in all his life would he have been able to show himself anywhere but as a treacherous and loathly knight, and, though it broke his heart to send her from him, La Belle Iseult loved him too well to have him so disgrace himself.

So they parted; and a sadder parting never had been in this world, for they knew with a sure and certain knowledge that never again would they be allowed to meet; and their hearts were full of a love and sorrow almost too great to be borne. With tears and kisses they said farewell, vowing each to be true to the other till death, and after.

So Sir Tristram rode away into Wales, and Queen Iseult being discovered by King Mark, was made to return to him, only to be made a prisoner in the great grim castle at Tintagel, where all day long she sat sad and lonely, looking out over the sea, and musing sadly on all the bitterness life had held for her and for her lover. And her husband, jealous, wrathful, never slackened his watch over her, night or day.

A harder lot was Iseult's than her lover's, for he had change and action to distract his thoughts, and all the excitement of battle; but she had nothing to do but sit and think on all that might have been, until her heart was near to breaking.

Meanwhile, Sir Tristram arrived in Wales and met the monster Urgan, a huge, hideous creature with no notion of fighting, or chivalry, for the moment he beheld Sir Tristram, he rushed upon him, and would have dashed him to the ground, but that Sir Tristram by good hap saw what was coming, and swerved aside so that the blow fell harmless. And while the giant roared with rage and mortification, and tried to recover his balance, Sir Tristram swiftly drew his sword, and swinging it lightly round his head, cut the monster's right hand clean off at the wrist with one sharp stroke.

Maddened by the pain, Urgan fumbled with his left hand until he drew from his belt a short steel dagger which had been tempered with sorcery, and springing on Sir Tristram they closed together, and long and fiercely they fought until the cliffs trembled with the struggle, and the ground was sodden with blood.

Great ado had Sir Tristram to avoid the huge bulk of the giant, and greater and greater grew the strain upon his strength, until a blow from him sent the giant rolling over in the gory mud. He was soon on his feet again, but the moment had given Sir Tristram time to get his breath. Then they closed again, and the blows fell faster and more furiously than ever. The giant's groans of rage and excitement might have been heard for miles around, while the earth flew about them until they could scarce be seen. Between every joint of their corslets the blood ran down in streams, but the sight only infuriated them the more.

At last, with a fierce roar between bitter laughter and pain, Urgan smote Sir Tristram with such fury that he cracked his shield in half, and then before Sir Tristram could recover himself he smote him again so that he would have killed him had not the blow by great good chance turned aside. But, turning aside as it did, it gave Sir Tristram the chance he coveted, and rushing in on the giant before he had recovered his foothold, he smote him with such force and skill that he cleft him clean through; and in his agony Urgan leapt so high in the air that he fell back over the edge of the cliff, and dropped heavily into the sea.

His task accomplished, Sir Tristram got into his ship again and sailed away, and as he passed Tintagel, where his unhappy love lay a prisoner in the castle, his heart felt like to break; and his yearning for her was so great, it seemed as though it must bring her to him in spite of her jailers.

But they were parted, those two, by a fate as strong as death. And she lay immured in her castle home, while he sailed on and on, not heeding nor caring whither he went, for all that he loved dwelt on that bleak iron-bound coast, as far from him as though the whole wide world lay between them.

And so at last, not heeding whither he sailed, he came to that sunny land where his wife Iseult dwelt, praying always for revenge because she had been scorned by him. On the coast at Brittany he landed, close by his own castle, but no sooner had he stepped ashore than he was met by a knight who knelt before him and besought his aid.

"Noble sir," cried he, "I am in sore distress. Some robbers, who infest this land like a scourge, met me as I was riding along with my new-made bride, and I being alone and single-handed, they quickly mastered me, and binding me, carried my bride away. And how to rescue her I know not. Come to my aid, sir, I beseech you, for you look a noble and trusty knight."

Sir Tristram, glad to have some distraction from his sorrow, was only too ready to help others who suffered for love's sake. So to Iseult he sent a message to say he had arrived, and would have been with her but for the quest, which he was bound to accomplish for his honour's sake, and for the sake of his knighthood. Then he departed, and he and the knight rode along the seashore in search of the robbers.

All night they slept in the wood by the sea, but as soon as morning broke there sounded close at hand a great trampling of horses and clanking of arms, and soon came along the robber band, with the pale-faced, terrified lady in their midst, fastened to one of the robbers.

At this sight the hapless young husband could no longer restrain himself. With a fierce cry he flew at the man to whom his bride was bound, while Sir Tristram, cool and strong, closed with the band and slew three before they had tried to defend themselves. And so the unequal battle began, and so it raged; but with so much courage and fierceness did the two knights fight for their just cause, that soon nearly all the robber band lay lifeless on the ground.

The young knight, though, was himself by that time wounded by the last remaining of the band, and ill would it have gone with him, for the reeking sword was raised high to give him the final blow, when Sir Tristram with a cry of triumph rushed in and clove the man so that he never breathed again.

Thus was all accomplished, and gladly was Sir Tristram returning on his homeward way, when one of the robbers who had made his escape and lay concealed, shot at Sir Tristram from his hiding-place, and the arrow pierced Sir Tristram in that same wound whereof he had nearly died before he went to Ireland, and La Belle Iseult cured him. And now he felt like to die again.

Scarcely could he stagger home through the long miles of that rugged forest by the sea; his eyes were faint and blinded, his legs shook under him. Parched, trembling, well-nigh dead, he reached at last his castle gates, but there his strength failed him, and with a terrible cry he fell prostrate on the ground.

At the sound forth came soldiers and servants, and strong men lifted him in kindly arms and laid him gently on a bed, calling aloud for someone to come and dress his wound.

Over by the window of the big hall sat Iseult la Blanche Mains, gazing with stony, unseeing eyes out over the golden sea, paying no heed to the noise and bustle going on about her. She had recognized that cry of pain at the gate, and knew her husband had returned sore stricken, but never, never once did she turn her head to look at him, nor move to give him comfort or assistance. And Tristram, ill though he was, felt the change in her manner to him, and grieved in his heart that all was not as it should have been, for he could not bear to cause pain to any woman.

As soon as he could speak he called to her, humbly, "Iseult, my wife!" At that she rose and went to him, but sullenly, and stood looking at him as though he were a stranger.

"Kiss me," he whispered, and at his bidding she stooped and kissed him, but it was as though an icicle had brushed his cheek, and a black cloud of misery settled down upon him, and despairing longing for her who would have been so gentle and kind to him; and towards his wife his heart hardened.

And she, poor little Iseult, her heart aching sorely with love and jealousy and bitter pain, returned to her seat, and no movement did she make to heal her lord of his wound, though she alone could do so. But in her heart she had vowed that she would not give him health and life torture me!"

"The sails are black," she answered in a cold, hard voice.

Then was the terrified woman sore afraid, for with a mighty effort Sir Tristram sprang from his bed, and took one step across the floor, and in a voice that made even her heart throb and bleed with pity, "Iseult—my love—my love!" he cried. Then a sudden darkness falling upon him, he flung out his arms as though to catch at something. "Iseult—Iseult—my love—come—to me!" he gasped in broken tones, and with a thud fell at his wife's feet, dead.

"I come, my love, I come!" rang out a sweet voice, full of love and tenderness and joy; and up the castle steps flew La Belle Iseult, and across the hall to where he lay. And never a look she gave at the pale, unhappy wife. Never a glance at aught beside that form.

"Tristram, my beloved! I am here. I am with you—with you for all time," she cried, flinging herself on her knees beside him. And never another word did she speak,—for when they raised her, her spirit had followed his to where none could part them more.

So died those two who had lived and loved so sadly and so truly. And when he was dead there was found round Sir Tristram's sword-belt the story of the fatal love-draught, and when he read it deep was the grief and bitter the remorse of King Mark that he had ever parted those two so bound together, and driven them to such despair.

Once more 'The Swan' sailed over the sea to Tintagel, and this time she bore Sir Tristram and his love together, for side by side they were to be buried in a dainty chapel made for them alone, that at last they should never more be parted.

But in time the sea, jealous for those lovers whose doom she had seen, came up and drew that dainty chapel into her own bosom. And there, where none can see them, the lovers sleep in peace for evermore, wrapped round and guarded by the blue waters of the deep Atlantic sea.

Printed in Great Britain
by Amazon

only that he might leave her again to go to that other Iseult. So, stern and cold she sat by the window looking out upon the sea, and never spake one gentle word, or tried to win his love.

And thus three days and nights passed by, and ever the husband and wife drifted more and more apart. Sir Tristram's wound refused to heal, his strength failed him more and more, but still his wife made no attempt to save him.

At last there came a day when Sir Tristram could no longer endure his lonely, loveless life, or his pain of mind and body, with never a kindly word or deed to comfort him. This hard, reproachful woman tortured him hour by hour with her sullen face and hard eyes, her cruel, cold indifference. And his love for that other Iseult, so tender, and true, and loving, burnt like fire in his veins and consumed him. So calling to him Ganhardine, his wife's brother, who loved him greatly, he bade him, by the love they bore each other, to take his ship 'The Swan,' and with all speed sail in her to England; and there to land at Tintagel, and by fair means or foul to convey to Queen Iseult the ring which he there gave him. To tell her, too, how that he, Sir Tristram, was like to die, but could not die in peace till he had seen her face once more.

"Then if it be that she comes, hoist a white sail that I may know my love still loves me, and is on her way. If not, then let the sail be black, that I may know, and die."

And Iseult of the White Hands heard each word he spake, and never a word she said; but her rage and jealousy well-nigh consumed her.

So Sir Ganhardine left upon his errand, and sailed for Tintagel in 'The Swan,' and the journey did not take him long, for the ship flew through the waters like a real bird, as though she knew she was bound on her master's errand, and that his life depended on her swiftness.

Dark it was when Ganhardine arrived, for it was winter-time, when storms rage full violent on that bleak coast. And at once he landed, and was made welcome by King Mark, for a stranger, and a noble one, was ever welcome in that lone country; and the king's heart never misgave him that this was a messenger from Sir Tristram.

Now it happened that Dame Bragwaine knew Sir Ganhardine, for they had been lovers in days gone by, and more than glad they were to see each other again. So with Bragwaine's gladly given help, Ganhardine conveyed Sir Tristram's ring to Queen Iseult in a cup of wine, so that when the queen drank, there at the bottom of the cup lay Sir Tristram's ring, one that she had given him long ago. And there she saw it, and her pale sad face lit up with such a wondrous joy that she had some ado to conceal her emotion from the king and those around her who were ever keeping her watched.

Deftly, though, she slipped the ring out of her mouth, and deftly she presently managed to slip it into her bosom, marvelling much the while whence and how it came, and why. And her anxiety and longing nigh drove her beside herself. For until all the inmates of the castle had retired to rest, naught could she learn of the mystery, or of the stranger who had come to the castle. But once within her own apartments, where she was no longer watched and guarded as of yore, she quickly, at Dame Bragwaine's bidding, muffled herself to the eyes, and creeping softly down a flight of secret stairs, she got out of the castle by a private passage-way and reached the spot where 'The Swan' lay moored, and where Sir Ganhardine awaited her with his message and his sad story.

When she heard tell of Sir Tristram's sad plight, and how that he was like to die, but could not die in peace till he had once more beheld her, there was no need to plead with her to leave all and go to him. Almost before the tale was told her she had stepped on board the ship, and without one glance behind her or one regret she set sail upon the stormy wintry sea to go to her true love, as fast as the faithful 'Swan' could carry her. And in her joy that once again she should be with him, once again she should see him, she almost forgot his sore plight, for hard it was for her to believe that Sir Tristram could be like to die.

Meanwhile death was drawing nearer and nearer to Sir Tristram. His restlessness aggravated his wound, his anxious, tortured mind increased his fever, so that truly he was like to die at any moment. And all the time, a little way from him sat White-handed Iseult, pale and cold without, the better to bide the burning rage within.

"Iseult! Iseult!" cried the sick man in his sleep.

"I am here. What would you?" she answered coldly, and he opened his eyes with a half-doubting joy in them; but his heart sank like lead, and all the joy died out of him, for the voice was not the voice of his love, nor the face her face, and sore wearily he sighed, and turned his face away.

"I wronged you past all forgiveness when I married you," he said, "for my heart had long been given to La Belle Iseult, whose sworn knight I was; but I did love you, I thought I could make you happy. Have you no pity? Can you feel no mercy for me now?" he cried piteously.

"I feel nothing," she answered bitterly; "between you, you have killed my heart, and all that was good in me."

So his heart yearned all the more for the gentler, more tender Iseult. Wearily he moved in his bed and watched for the first gleam of daylight. Slowly the hours dragged by, relieved only by the plash, plash of the waves against the castle walls, or the sighs of the sick man.

Then within a while he spoke again. "My wife," he said, "when morning comes, look across the sea, and tell me if you see a ship coming, and if its sails be black or white, that I may the sooner be out of this miserable uncertainty."

Obediently she rose, and sat watching until the first ray of dawn, when, skimming over the sea through the morning mist, she saw the dainty 'Swan,' with her white sails like wings gleaming through the dimness. Over the wide waters she flew, until she drew close to the castle, and the anchor was cast. Then from out her sprang Ganhardine, and following quickly after him came La Belle Iseult. Too impatient to wait for help she sprang lightly on the shore, and stood there breathless, eager, glad.

And so for the first time Iseult la Blanche Mains saw that other Iseult, and as she stood on the shore in her white gown, with her golden hair falling out under her hood like a mantle over her shoulders, the unhappy wife marvelled not that Tristram loved so fair a creature, and her heart sank at sight of her beauty, and fiercer burnt her jealousy.

"They come," she said sullenly, turning to her husband.

"Ah!" he cried, with a deep groan of intolerable suspense. "Of thy mercy tell me, and do not